Life Below Decks

G. P. Wayne

For the Arvon Foundation,
who led me to water...

Contents

Bad Barnet   7

Official Versions   26

Agrippa   45

Pepi's pizza   56

Life Below Decks   58

The Chicken's Progress   77

Famous Sword   97

Donkey Rides   112

Courage and Convictions   116

Long Legs of the Law   133

Men Play the Game, Women Know the Score   150

Just Like the Real Thing   167

Mysterious Ways   182

Bad Barnet

I only stopped off at Patrick's Sporting Club to get the bastard off my back. A different bastard mind you: Patrick: long gone, well before my time. These days, the owner's a sly Bangladeshi known as Armtwister Ali, mainly due to the way he would stick to his opponents like a leech rather than duke it out.

That was years back. Don't get me wrong – I've always had time for Ali, but this little trip was verging on the ridiculous. He'd been calling me for weeks, leaving endless messages, generally just being a right pain in the arse.

The gist of it was this: Ali had a prospect he thought could be a decent little earner – not long term, but what you might call a fixed return, one shot and out – and more or less begged me to drop by with one of my boys for a demo.

Now it was logical that Ali would want me in, since I had the setup he needed to put the money down without attracting attention, but as with all deals, you do have to have a product – at least one that stands enough scrutiny to fool the punters. And as usual, there was a catch: as useful product goes, Ali wasn't the kind of trainer you'd expect to have one.

If it hadn't been for the fact that one of my best boys, a Gambian we called Jimmy Akimbo – nobody could pronounce his real name without losing teeth – had to do the medical ready for an outing in Tottenham, I never would have stopped by Patrick's. But you know how it is; the Board examiner's gaff was just round the corner, and after the cursory prod and poke and a fucking great fee, I couldn't bring myself to drive right past Ali's place without calling in.

Soft, ain't I?

Truth is, I was hoping that by calling unannounced, either Ali or his prospect (or both) might not be around, so later I could tell Ali to fuck off while pointing out I had made the effort, blaming him or his boy for their failure to be in the right place, etcetera.

Best laid plans, eh? As I pushed open the grimy green door and started up the stairs with a puzzled but obedient Akimbo in tow, Ali appeared on the landing with a huge grin and half a doner in one mitt.

"Pirate Pete. You bring me a sacrifice too. How nice. Come up, oh yes, do come right up."

Always was a cheeky git.

Calling Patrick's a gym was just taking the piss. It has the smell – sweat and medicinal – but mixed in with bad drains, dead rats and mould. Hard to believe damp could rise that high. Sure, there was a ring, floor-bound, the ropes frayed and sagging, the canvas patched with gaffer tape. An old bag hung dejectedly in one corner, beaten to death, stuffing a bulge in the middle shaped like its owner. A few chipped weights hung along one wall, beneath which was a contraption a mate of Ali's had sold him, swearing blind it was a Nautilus prototype. Jules fucking Verne more like, something a plumber would put together as a joke from parts nicked out of a scrapped lift and the remains of a canoe.

That was it – no speedball, dip frame, crunch bench – all gone now. The whole place was dingy, flaky paint etcetera, badly lit by a single strip light over the ring. There were other lights, but it was a toss-up whether Ali was too cheap to turn them on or if they actually worked at all.

"So, you are coming to try out my boy. I am delighted, truly." Ali eyed Akimbo up and down, the smallest gleam of professional interest lighting his eyes for a second, before age and disillusion dimmed them again, leaving only the usual sly calculation. "Good choice. A division up, but that is of no consequence. Wait here please; I will get my boy."

Ali walked to the back and disappeared through a door I could barely see. I grinned at Akimbo. "Fancy a snack?" My boy showed a very predatory row of bright white teeth, some of which he might retain if I can just get him not to stand there and admire his handiwork after landing a good punch. He said something that might have been "you want me to fight now?" but I couldn't be bothered to explain. He'd get the idea when Ali brought in his prospect.

Akimbo liked drawing his name in the claret, and was always delighted when the opportunity presented itself. Game little bastard, and not without skill either. Truth is, for something like this, in ordinary circumstances I would have brought one of my chimps rather than the Gambian, but like I said, it was just convenient timing.

The door down the end squeaked and Ali came back in. Behind him came the boy, and I had to laugh. He was all decked out like he was walking down the aisle at Bethnal Green surrounded by heavies, with fucking Rocky playing loud in the background. Gown, boots, gloves already laced and taped, and sweaty, like he'd been warming up. Dear oh dear. Was I supposed to be fooled by some water sprinkled on his bleedin' forehead, for fuck's sake? I glanced at my boy. He wasn't smiling now, but had the hard look I like to see on a fighter.

Trailing behind Ali like a damp dog, the kid stepped into the light. Thin, that's what I remember most. Scrawny. I've seen devastating flys and bantams who look like stick insects but can land punches so heavy you want to check their gloves for weights. But this one just looked like he'd escaped from a refugee camp or a Dickens book.

The barnet was the scariest thing about him. He had the worst haircut I've ever seen on anything two-legged. His knees were like two knobbly mutant potatoes. At this moment, instead of putting my boy in the ring with this urchin, I wanted to get in there myself with Ali so I could punch his fucking lights out. Well and truly out, wasting my time like this. I would have left right then too, if Akimbo hadn't already got too much of the red mist about him to take him back into the street.

And something else: a stillness. Thinking about it, it wasn't so much that Ali's boy didn't jitter or float, or jog on the spot to keep the circulation going and the muscles warm. He wasn't doing any of that. He just wasn't moving *at all*.

It wasn't a lack of nerves nor lack of attention neither. His eyes were sharp, bright, but they were the only thing about him that moved; the rest of 'im was like a scrawny reject from Madame Tussauds after they ran out of wax. It seemed like every time I glanced away, he would look at someone else. I never actually saw him move, like he waited until I wasn't looking before he turned his head. Even when I spoke to him, said hello or whatever, he ignored me and continued to stare at Akimbo – not in a hostile way I might add, more kinda curious – as he said hello back. (At least I think that's what he said).

I checked out my boy to see how he was taking it, and when I turned back the urchin was staring at me, unflinching but blank. Nothing except the stare, and you couldn't really tell what he was looking at, or what he was seeing. I didn't care for it much either way; and then I was glad I had brought Akimbo after all.

Another thing I think about is how quiet Ali was. Most times, when someone's touting a prospect, they do the Don King thing: motor mouths, talking trash and laying it on with a trowel. Doesn't matter if the prospect is the next champ or a drug-addled dickhead, the volume level of the verbal diarrhoea is always the same. Yet Ali was as silent as his boy was motionless, just stood there while the rest of us eyed each other up. Actually, I think he was impatient.

"This is Viktor," he finally announced. "You would like to see him do some work?"

I shook my head; may as well get it over with as quick as poss. A speedball workout will reveal clues to the experienced eye, but Ali didn't have one – speedball that is – and punching a bag means bugger all considering they haven't invented one yet that will pin you on the ropes and beat your lungs into jelly.

Ali didn't bother to hide the fact he was pleased. "Right then," he said, too cheerful by half, and nodded at Viktor, who climbed through the ropes. I would have given Akimbo the nod but he was already half way through himself, his track top dumped on the floor. (I do like a boy that's keen, always ready to do the business). As Viktor shrugged off his fancy robe I couldn't stop myself laughing. He had his name embroidered on the back in gold thread – can't remember the surname but it was foreign, east European – and above it the moniker 'Viktorious'. Just the one word. I wondered if his mum had done the needlework. Pretender to the throne, and don't forget to pull the chain. It was all a bit silly, to be frank.

So silly in fact that I saw Akimbo was ready to beat on the boy with his bare hands – and his Tottenham bout only a week away for fuck's sake. I whistled to him and motioned him over to one corner, more or less holding him there while I helped him into his gloves. As I tied them up I glanced behind my boy to see Viktor standing in the opposite corner, so still it was a bit weird. It reminded me of something that wouldn't come; I couldn't pay that much attention while I was busy with the laces.

Job done, I stood back. Ali came over to stand beside me. "Defence only," he called out to his boy. "No punching…yet." I would have asked him what he was playing at but Akimbo was already advancing. Viktor was on his toes now, and I swear he was vibrating from head to foot, shivering like a yearling after a run. He didn't look cold though. Or nervous. Quite the opposite; he looked bored, which I thought was a bit off.

So did Akimbo, evidently. Thing about him; while he ain't no twinkle-toes, he has all the right moves. Good footwork, nice weight shift, gets the punches loaded up proper. He just seems to plod round the ring, neither graceful nor pretty. Fast though, but not, as it turns out, fast enough. Without ceremony, he chucks a few jabs out but can't get the range. He combos, I see the arms moving but I don't hear the contact, just wind and grunting.

It isn't like the kid is running away either. I look down at Viktor's feet and I'm mesmerised. I never saw such economy, such exact footwork. None of the Tyson crouch or bendy torso, just small movements. No pattern of bobbing and weaving, just the exact reaction required to evade the incoming, and nothing more.

My pulse rate shot up. I glance at Ali, who's looking at his stopwatch, and when I look back, Akimbo is trying to cut down the ring and get the boy into a corner where he can do some damage. The approach was faultless as far as I could see, cunning like, cutting off any escape. But I notice Viktor watching very carefully, and when he gets the measure of the pattern – all boxers develop patterns of attack, mostly to their cost later on – he was gone. Just gone, dancing a little in the opposite corner and waiting like a beggar between begs.

OK, so he was fast and slippery. You can only play that record for so long before the needle slips and the wheels come off. You get tagged in the end, and if the first punch slows you down while you try to clear your head and stay out of trouble – assuming the legs haven't gone already – the second will murder you because any decent boxer will have the range measured and the tempo well marked. The double-tap, instinctive.

But like he'd read my mind, the spider boy didn't wait for Akimbo to lumber over: he dances over to meet him. Fucking cheek, inviting him on like that. Snot-nosed kid taking the piss out of a decent pro like the Gambian.

I could see Akimbo had wrapped hisself up in the cold clarity it had taken so long to get ingrained. When he first came to me, the red mist came down like Noah's flood and drowned the bugger, so I put him in to spar with some really good punchers and told them to wind him up and knock him down, up and down, up and down. After a few weeks of this, it started to dawn on the big ebony hulk that his anger and lust for violence was getting him in trouble. It's what being a professional fighter is all about; not acting like a brawler on the piss but controlled, accurate, measured. Boxing is about the ebb and flow of the fight, waiting, moving, positioning and probing. When the tide turns, you have to go with it, commit, but before then it is about keeping your head. Careful and deadly: disciplined, in other words. Mind you, I've seen title contenders forget every bit of that sage advice, even after thirty or more pro fights. And get slaughtered, usually by hard-nut Cubans or Mexicans who eat rusty nails for breakfast wrapped in a ground-glass tortilla.

So now my boy is stalking, deadly serious. He tries everything, but nothing lands. Jabs slip away; uppercuts keep going up and away like his gloves are filled with helium; hooks miss by millimetres. He tries several times to clinch the kid so he can tuck into his kidneys, but can't quite catch hold of him. Akimbo is breathing hard now, partly because he didn't warm up first, and partly because punches that don't connect are very tiring; wasted effort that combines with the frustration, eating away at discipline and energy like acid.

"Time," Ali calls out, clicking his stopwatch. Viktor turns his back on Akimbo instantly and walks away, leaving my boy frozen in mid punch. For a moment, I thought he was going to hit the kid in the back of the head and I wouldn't have blamed him, neither. I called out and he came over, shaking his big head and scowling etcetera.

"Well, at least he ain't hit you neither, son. That round's a draw," I told him (perhaps a little unconvincingly, truth be told). "Do your work, and remember this is just a private little do, not a fucking title fight, all right?"

Nothing. Not a glimmer.

"You hear me mate? No money, get me? You listening?"

My boy nods reluctantly and turns round. Viktor is doing the tree bit again, his chest barely moving. Good fitness, and clearly a miser with his energy. Nothing wrong with that either, it's just not good show-business to appear to put in so little effort. Dismissive too, though if it winds up your opponent it's an asset, of course. Clever little bastard.

As Akimbo moves forward, I see Viktor look at Ali, who gives him the nod. The fighters close with me staring at my boy's back, a big slab of black rippled marble. He turns to the left as Viktor starts to circle him. I get a clear look at what happens next – that is, I can see what I can't see, but hear all too well – I don't see the punches land, but I hear the staccato pattern of leather on flesh and it is frighteningly fast (which is why I can't really see it). Ribs, stomach, below the heart, more ribs, then, like a machine gun ranging upwards from the recoil, the hands travel up the body. I see one uppercut go in that rocks my boy on his heels and I stop breathing, waiting for the finish, but Viktor steps back, the straight arm follow-up arrested in mid-flight. He glances over at Ali and me, big eyes twinkling. Now *this* is show-business.

He looks at us too long though. Out of the corner of my eye I see Akimbo lunge at Viktor, blindsiding him. I swear Viktor smiles a tiny smile at us as he pulls his head back and lets the punch sail harmlessly past his nose, *without even looking at Akimbo*. And that's when I remembered what his stillness reminded me of: a martial artist. I'd seen a few demonstrations in my time, some of the Bruce Lee home movie stuff and quite a bit of karate and tai quan do (fucking brutal, those bastards) but what I liked best were the 'soft' forms, even though they are based on the notion you would never start a fight, just finish it. It's all about some kind of inner calm, the absence of any rush, just observation from that still centre that slows down time and allows you to use the opponent's energy against him without hardly using any of your own.

Same as I was saying, really. That's what the boy had, that contained, almost placid confidence that required no flash, no thunder, no waste of precious energy or time. Just the coopy de grass, no fuss or fanfare: as Akimbo's treacherous – and failed – attack carries his body forward, the spider steps back and clips him as he passes – almost 'take that with you' nonchanlance. Not a big punch, but so bloody accurate it makes me wince. Didn't seem to be much effort in it, not much shoulder, except that the sweat that shoots off my boy's head from the impact is travelling real fast, almost as fast as Akimbo's pole-axed body falls to the floor. Not a KO exactly, but no way would he beat a count after that little lot.

Viktor was already back in his corner and had his robe on, but still watching Akimbo, which I thought was smart. I didn't need to see any more, obviously, and now there was business to do with Ali, so we called out to the fighters to shake and my boy does me proud when he embraces the stick insect and pats him on the back. He was generous, was my Gambian boy – dead now, shot in a drive-by in Peckham by crackheads he owed money to. Fucking idiot.

Viktor smiled for the first time (for certain) before climbing out of the ring to disappear the way he came. Ali looked at me expectantly, but I said nothing for a while. On paper, I should have been thrilled by the skill on display, but frankly it left me cold, chilled in fact. The whole thing was so dispassionate, so uninvolved. Clinical, that's the word I'm looking for, like surgery. Silent, no heavy breathing and no excitement, although I must admit the thought of all that money to be made tightened up the old ball bag a bit, know what I mean?

Akimbo lost the Tottenham fight, his confidence shattered by the stick insect taking him apart – he just couldn't get over it. Afterwards, I started to make the arrangements, which were pretty straightforward. First off, we needed a legend, as the spookies call it. I knew a dealer in Victoria – a real one, gun under the sofa and blocks of hash like paving stones – who got all his gear from the Lewisham Ruskies. Apparently, they were keen to help – for a fee, naturally – so the dealer made the arrangements and I put a monkey down – half in advance, half on delivery – and over the next few weeks Viktor started getting a few hits on Google as the Russian wiz kids got going. Nothing silly, just a mention planted in some Lativan local on-line paper, a couple of faked results on Polish no-name amateur cards, something complementary hacked into some long-retired Estonian boxer's unattended web site, some photoshopped pictures of the same awful barnet on a slightly younger head (how do they do that – make people look younger?) and a rather cute reference to an illegal immigrant charge made by the frog police in Calais against someone whose name was nearly (but not quite) the same, on some blog about free movement between EU countries – a nice touch, I thought. Enough for the bookies to chew on, but nothing to make them choke.

Over the next three months I got him on five decent cards, the last two with modest local and trade press coverage, just a results listing, nothing more. Cost a few bob, as did the license, but we needed some form before the bookies would bother to notice. The kid was a breeze, did exactly what he was told and produced one win, a draw and then three losses, none of which were fought ineptly. You wouldn't have known him from the contained fighter I had seen that day though. Ragged, over-excited, rushing around like an idiot one minute, sullen and lethargic the next. It was a good act.

After that, I was pleased to see him given odds – bloody long ones – at my local bookies before the last fight, which he lost on points after a scrappy defence against a world-weary pro who just wanted to finish the bout and get down the pub with a couple of folding ponies in his back pocket to treat his mates and brag about the job he'd done on the kid.

Then we put him in with a terrible ponce called Mickey Spiller, who couldn't punch his way out of a paper bag, but had money behind him put up by his dad, a builder who knew as much about boxing as I did about studwork – less actually, since it's a good place to stash stuff. Viktor decimated him, really took him apart, and he was clever going about it. It all looked rather accidental somehow, even the knockout, which came towards the end of the fifth with every round going to the kid up till then. He did just enough to be convincing, but not so much that he looked like he could step up against serious opposition.

The payday was set up against a class act – Lenny Lumbago, we called him, on account of his back trouble – his real name was Lumumba, as I recall. Something like that. He was a good choice because he had survived several operations to fix his back and needed something easy to chew on before getting in the ring with anything wicked.

Lenny was an out-fighter; tall, rangy, had arms the length of Nelson's column, could handle himself well and worked at distance. He didn't have what you'd call a really big punch but he was versatile - could tuck in so there was nothing on offer, get close and hammer away with tidy inside work, sapping up punches with his arms and gloves, then step quickly back on his toes to throw ferocious long range bombs that found their way between opponents defences like his gloves were coated in Teflon. (He let his hands drop too much for my liking, but all the flash fighters do it nowadays for a bit of bragging).

This was the delicate bit of the plan. I had to let Ali set up the fight because Lenny's manager was remotely connected to the Givens mob, and you fucked with them at your extreme peril (I'm one of the few who ever got away with it as it happens, but that's another story). I asked Ali about it, if he was scared of any blowback. He just asked me if I realised how big India was. No idea, I told him.

What I never said was that I didn't give a toss. It was entirely his problem, so long as he got the deal and never mentioned me. Someone told me later that the only way Ali could have pulled it off was if he clued in Lenny's manager and got him to bet against his own boy, which makes sense because it would insulate Ali from any retribution. Sounds likely: in this game, nothing surprises me.

We got ours down early, just in case. All over the country we had solid, dependable punters with enough savvy to keep their bets modest even though they knew which way a race or a fight would go. Takes a lot of time, all the screening with test tips to find out if they send all the money promptly – less their cut, obviously. (The laggards are the ones who are going to fuck with you later, make you send up a car loaded with baseball bats and people who know how to do damage with them).

Anyway, dependability means not taking the piss and going bonkers, suddenly chucking ten grand on the counter in William Hill's at 200-1. There is nothing that interests the Commission more than a few big wins on a complete unknown with no form, or a big prospect who falls down in mysterious circumstances. Fighters aren't any good at acting, not like footballers. I've seen fighters throw a fight so badly, the punters were laughing too hard to boo.

The long and the short of it is that we had a really nice solid plunger set up, even supplying a bit of dosh here and there for them to lose on long-odds rubbish at their target bookies (not their usual, don't want to fuck up their leisure time and make enemies from punters along the counter – that's another way to get done). To get set up, you pop in to a bookies half a dozen times and put a pony or two on something long and bleedin' unlikely; they remember you – another mad bastard in a world generally stuffed with shuffling grey men pouring over the form of horses they can't even be bothered to watch on the close circuit TV.

The bookies like my mad punters because they don't put down loads of tiny bets, just one or two biggies. They know you might get lucky some time – all in the odds I guess – so they don't complain when you bring one home either; you'll be back soon enough so they can take your winnings off you, with interest. A couple of grand payout don't bother them; it's fifty and upwards that makes them anxious and reticent to cough up without making a few calls first, unless they know you. Betting on an uncertain outcome? No chance: I leave that shit to the gamblers of this world.

I think at this point we had about seventy-five grand down in the UK, and the same abroad. Generally we were getting tasty odds, nothing extravagant but it was lining up to be a good earner all round.

Ali hadn't come up with his money yet – 30K – which we had already committed for him. I tried every number I had, but I couldn't get hold of him. We did find the boy, training at Patrick's on his own between shards of glass and bits of broken door. The gym had been broken into, although what anyone thought they could half-inch out of that dump was beyond me. I put my wing-man Dan on the case and told him to clean up the gaff, put the boy through his paces, keep curious punters away and an eye out for Ali.

Stuck in traffic outside the Beckett in the Old Kent Road, my moby did the dance in my pocket. It was Ali, sounding frightened. "They stole my stake," he whined. On the hands free he sounded like he was crying in a tunnel. I shrugged, watching a big ugly woman beating a dog on the pavement outside the dry cleaners as I crawled toward the Elephant and Castle at two miles an hour.

"You still got time," I told him. The dog bit the woman and I gave a silent cheer.

"I'm hiding, Pete. I am afraid, well afraid, innit?..." I waited, sensing he would get on with it if I didn't interrupt him and I was right as usual. (I'm good at sussing people out).

"It wasn't my money," was all he said, but I caught on straight away. He'd borrowed his stake, probably from the Southall mob. Absolute madness; the Southall Asians were generally OK with us, probably because they were outnumbered, but mainly because race-wars are really fucking expensive, disrupting loads of good business. Nobody wants that kind of disturbance, and very ugly it is too. But amongst themselves they were completely unscrupulous. It occurred to me straight away that they probably followed Ali after he'd picked up the cash, watched where he stashed it, and lifted it the second his back was turned. Double payday: fucking ruthless, those boys.

Now in case you're wondering, I don't lend Ali any more money. Not fucking likely. I already feel really stupid having put down his stake before he came up with cash, but an operation like this is inflexible, a machine; you put out the plan and hundreds of people do what they are told, when they are told, silent and anonymous. No changing orders because there's no contact, not after the instructions go out disguised as marketing emails, white print on a white background below the Viagra, holidays and insurance for old gits. Copy and paste and voila – the instructions to be learned and burned (always empty your bloody Recycle Bin, that's all I have to say about it).

So now I have a problem because I've commissioned 30K of bets for him like the daft cunt I am and Ali isn't covering it, *and* he's in for the same amount with the Paki mafia. (In my mitigation, as the briefs say, may I remind you that it was Ali's fighter in the first place, and Ali *did* bring the deal to me instead of Gary fucking Givens).

I'm at the New Kent Road flyover now in the wrong bleedin' lane – 300 yards in thirty minutes. Ali is still moaning down the tunnel so I cut him off. All I can think about is how much Viktor *had* to win the fight.

It was a nervy couple of days up to the fight, but thank God the bookies didn't pull the plug. Word was out, most of it bollocks, but Viktor's odds had shortened considerably. Didn't matter much to me, of course, since my bets were tight. I just didn't like all the stuff at the edges, frayed and distracting. Didn't hear from Ali again; no surprises there.

Main thing was the kid; he was working hard and, according to Dan, ready to do the business. I trust Dan, an experienced cutman who knows his stuff, been in the game longer than I have and a real artist with the end-swell and a dab of epinephrine. Used to work for Givens as it happens, back when Givens managed Ali. (Dan has to work under a different name these days, but we don't need to go into that).

On the scales, both came in nicely with Viktor giving away a couple of pounds to Lenny, who came in a whisker under the 122 pound junior feather limit without having to take off his shorts, much to the disappointment of the tarts like Given's wife Kelly, who turn up at every weigh-in hoping to see the boxers strip off. When they are that close to the limit, even the weight of their underpants may tip them over.

Lenny looked to be in good nick, relaxed and toned, although I suspected he might have worked hard to keep his weight down, with the intention of stepping up a division once he'd got the warm-up out of the way (which is exactly what he did). Lenny looked down his nose at Viktor, who was a couple of inches shorter, and when the time came for the eyeball stuff he was disdainful, trying to provoke the kid. Viktor just smiled like a corpse and walked away, leaving Lenny and his crew rather put out.

Dan was nervous. He knew the score and how much everything depended on the boy coming good. Bear in mind he hadn't seen what I'd seen, and I wouldn't let him take any of the chimps over to spar because they had gobs the size of the Blackwall tunnel and it was too close for silly risks, etcetera. So all Dan had to go on was just a few days' work with the rope, the saggy bag, the hook and jab pads and a floor-mounted speedball that Dan retrieved from his loft, last used by our 'enry hisself, if Dan was to be believed. Funny thing, that – Dan would tell us stories about his time with the septics but nobody believed him. One Christmas I popped in with some flowers and chocs for Dan's missus – she was ill for a long time and died a few weeks later, Ivy was her name – and I had a quick wet while she powdered her nose (makeup, that is). As Dan busied himself behind his little bar, I picked up a gaudy card from the mantelpiece and bugger me if it wasn't from Leon Spinks.

"Get one every year," Dan said indifferently as he gave me a half pint of Remy. "Saved his bacon that night. Still waiting for the fucking fee though."

I knew what was bothering him. He didn't like the look of Lenny's proven skills versus Viktor's lack of experience.

"I know how much you need this one Pete," he told me as we got in the car, like he was trying to warn me. Viktor was silent in the back. "It's just...well, it's a big ask, that's all. Anything can happen in the ring, you know that. And Lumbago ain't to be taken lightly. He looked the business to me". He glanced back at Viktor, who gave us both the Chinese – fucking inscrutable – and said nothing, just looked away out the window. To this day I don't know if the kid even spoke English.

He knew what to do though, and it was the Viktor I saw that first afternoon who climbed into the ring, mum's embroidery an' all. He was sweaty again, but this time from a punishing warm-up Dan and I could not believe, but didn't feel inclined to interrupt. The boy was focused like a needle; I don't think he even noticed the utter indifference of the crowd as we walked out. They did clap when Lenny emerged a few minutes later, but not for long – too busy getting lubricated in readiness for the top of the card, welterweight between a Welsh thug and an Irish thug and a toss-up whether the best action would be in the ring or beside it.

Formalities dispensed with, the bell rang and for the next quarter of an hour I witnessed the most beautiful boxing I had ever seen, save the greats. Talk about a rough diamond; there have been few times in my life when I've regretted a caper, but for a moment there I felt ashamed, imagining the thrill and pleasure of developing a talent like this, polishing it to the kind of perfection that makes dreams come true. So to say the dream came crashing down is another way of describing what happened to Viktor, because all of a sudden he was lying on the canvas, out cold.

Basically, he won the first four rounds by a mile. You could see the consternation in Lenny's corner after the first round, when it had dawned on them that Viktor was something very special. His movement was a wonder, for instance: the pace kept changing, fast then slow, making it hard to predict where to aim. Turns, reverses, in and out – just lovely, like a ballet dancer with some serious violence. He was landing punches too, hard ones out of nowhere, flurries in your face.

Lenny was doing dick and looking sick as a dog. At the end of the second, he had a bruise over one eye and was rubbing his back on the way to the stool. Dan grinned. "Getting his excuses ready, I reckon," he muttered as he sponged down the unmarked boy. In the fourth, Viktor landed a right-hook so perfectly timed it made the crowd – now paying attention – gasp as one. Lenny was backpedalling, stalling while his legs came back and I thought Viktor was going to finish him off but the bell rang.

Another funny thing was the silent corner work. Usually everyone and his bleedin' uncle has advice for the fighter between rounds (I've even had daft gits in the audience ring my moby between rounds to tell me what we're doing wrong – can you believe that shit?)

Not this time. Viktor was in such control that I couldn't think of anything to say that wasn't stating the bleedin' obvious. Dan muttered a few things, keep your guard up etcetera, but mostly we just wiped and watered and waited for the next bell. I had no doubt about the outcome, which made what happened next all the more shocking.

Like Dan said, Lenny Lumbago was not to be taken lightly. Cutting to the chase, after a bit of testing either way, he simply moved his eyes one way and his shoulders the other, landed a really good hook right on the kid's jaw, his uppercut arriving a quarter-second later like the pro he is. Tap fucking tap. And that, as they say, was that.

I had the 150 grand all right, but covering the losses pretty much bankrupted me. More's the point, nobody would work with me again after making such a blunder, even though they'd made a mint out of me previously. My other prospects quit and went elsewhere. Dan buggered off, I think in disgust at the whole thing; the boy vanished like smoke, Ali never resurfaced and I went to ground. A lot of people were said to be pissed off with me, so it was months before I dared show my face in my local boozer.

Turned out I'd been keeping low for nothing; there had been no comeback after the fight, no bad blood that anyone knew about, and nobody had been asking after me. One odd thing: Dan was rumoured to have paid off his mortgage, although where he'd get the dosh for that kind of caper is anyone's guess – mine was that since he had no faith in the kid, he'd put money down on Lenny. Nobody had seen Ali and Viktor was never mentioned.

Anyway, all that was a year back. I'm out of the game now, got a nice little earner from a pitch in the East Lane market, prime spot at the Walworth Road end. We knock out these brooms, mops etcetera coming in from Africa and India with the handles full of ivory blanks we sell to dodgy piano makers.

This particular morning was quiet. I was across the road getting some folding from the Barclays hole in the wall next to the site of the old Carter Street nick – no, I lie; that's a block down the road, I'm on the corner of Penrose Street – when my name is called out. I look behind me and there's Givens in his Merc and his gold-rimmed glasses, cruising up towards the Elephant like the ponce he is. The man beside him looked away sharpish, but I could see he was Asian. As Givens pulled off with nothing more than a sly nod, I saw he also had a passenger in back. Couldn't see the face through the tinted glass, just the spiky outline of a an unmistakably bad barnet.

Official Versions

I don't fit the profile, do I? Not abused as a child, no violent men beating me, no hardships. My family were middle class – dad worked as an insurance assessor, mum was a primary school supply teacher. Their marriage was steady, placid, dutiful.

I was pretty straight, looking back. Did my homework, didn't have much to do with drugs (although I always liked a drink, but not in excess). Didn't pop my cherry until I was nineteen, which made me look a bit like a novice nun or something. The other girls used to call me 'Sister Andrea' but they weren't cruel about it. I think they rather envied my innocence in some strange way.

After I split up with Phillip, I was at a complete loss. No money, nowhere to live, no career or prospects. I thought about going back to complete my degree, but I couldn't support myself because I was made redundant from my secretary's job: no place for secretaries these days, a dying breed. You have no idea how high the odds are stacked against a woman approaching middle age, believe me. What did I have to show for eight years of marriage? Absolutely nothing, my love. Nothing at all.

It's funny when you look back and notice all the signs you were deliberately blind to for so long. I wonder now how I could have convinced myself to leave uni and marry Phillip, but that's exactly what I did. *Mrs. Andrea Goodhall* – I didn't feel demeaned by taking his name; it was what I wanted.

Respectability and security. I never felt safe when I left home. The other girls at uni were OK, but I felt a bit aloof from them, not that they were against me or anything, or even unkind. It was just that I didn't know what I really wanted, and they all did – or seemed to. I was intimidated by their sense of direction, of purpose and ambition, their independence.

They were not radical as such, just bloody determined. I was not. I wasn't even sure what I was doing at uni – it was just the thing I was supposed to do after doing reasonably well at school. So when I met Phillip after a talk he gave on local government, I was probably primed for what followed.

I have a habit of talking about myself in a demeaning way. Same lack of confidence, I expect. Do we ever really change? I make it sound like Phillip was just an escape route for a scared little girl, but that wasn't it at all. Actually, it was sex.

Phillip Goodhall was 26 when I met him. He was on fire; the rough edges had been sanded off by four years of local political activism, but he was still the idealist, the young proto-Marxist with a curious conviction that socialism could be bolted on to a capitalist system. He was convincing without being suave, fluent without being smooth. There was a kind of truth about him – I know this all sounds rather too naive – but believe me, you could tell he believed what he said, just like you could tell he was going somewhere.

After the talk, he had a drink with the organising committee, all fawning and batting their eyelashes so hard you could feel the breeze down the other end of the bar. I wasn't part of that clique, but as I ordered my drink, Phillip came up to the bar and stood next to me as he got in his round. Our eyes met, and he gave me a smile that made my legs shiver. We chatted briefly and when the drinks arrived, he picked them all up, except one. As he turned away I told him he'd missed it and he grinned.

'I didn't miss it. That's mine,' he said. 'I need an excuse to come back in a second'.

For the rest of the evening, he ignored the others and talked only to me. About everything. I remember exactly how much force came off him. I thought I was melting. There was kindness too, and generosity, but the main thing is how much he made me laugh, made me relax and feel worthy. I had all his attention, and it went to my head. After that, it went to other parts. I don't do lurid details, but let me tell you that I've never met another man who could give me so much pleasure, and I'm ashamed to say that when I look back on it, I wonder if I really fell in love with Phillip, or his astonishing techniques. If only I'd known then quite how many astonishing techniques he really had, and how widely he employed them.

Christ, I know I sound dumb, but I was twenty-one, for God's sake; narrow-minded, a little scared and with few worldly experiences behind me. I knew very little about life and I was simply overwhelmed by a man who seemed to have done everything there was to do already, even at his age. I longed for security and a home; a relationship with Phillip offered it on a gold plate, complete with all the trimmings. We were married nine months later, had a honeymoon in Hawaii and spent the whole two weeks fucking each other's brains out. I'm a fast learner my love, believe me.

There's a Latin proverb I heard once that made my stomach sink. It's this: *corruptio optimi pessima*. It means, 'the corruption of the best, is the worst'. Clever huh? It sums up how I felt watching what happened to Phillip.

When I married him, he was the best, the smartest, the brightest, the sexiest. Then came the drugs – cocaine mostly. We had these parties; nothing too big, because we were still living in a little two up two down Phillip was renting in Camberwell. (Turns out the house was owned by Gary Givens, but I'll come to that).

Thing is, coke was fashionable among the cerebral types that Phillip used to socialise with; business owners, a few local party workers and a few more from the Labour HQ in the Walworth Road, some trade union types, women from the local Feminist workshop, a sprinkling of black party activists and Muslim community workers, a handful of charitable do-gooders – I don't mean that unkindly – some teachers who couldn't discuss anything but teaching, and a stray musician or artist here and there, invited for colour and variety.

The parties started dragging on into the night, always with the same hardcore of coke snorting, wide-eyed demagogues arguing endlessly about topics that changed as fast as the coke disappeared. That was when Phillip started spending too much money on the stuff. He was working in the city at that time, at a commercial bank – an irony he enjoyed, I think, given his Marxist aspirations. 'Know your enemy,' he used to tell me. I should have listened.

So despite him having a decent salary, we were often broke. I didn't mind too much; the sex was still wonderful and I got a job as a secretary to make ends meet. Then one weekend, Gary Givens turned up uninvited. I didn't like him at all, but as Phillip's wife, the spouse of an up and coming politician, you have certain duties to perform, so I fed him and listened to him swear his way through several anecdotes, all of which left me feeling a little nauseated.

Towards the end of the evening we were rather drunk – Givens doesn't like the white powder that much so we stuck to the booze – and the talk turned to money. Phillip was pretty candid about our state of affairs, and Givens picked up on it. 'I have an acquaintance you should meet' he said. 'His name is Max, and he might be able to...' He tailed off, looked at me, and said no more. I ignored the implication, as I did the little chat they had at the end of the hall before Givens left.

I ignored the implication. None so blind...?

Two nights later, I came home from the gym early because I'd sprained my wrist. As I let myself in I heard voices; Phillip, and another man with a heavy East European accent. I didn't mean to spy on them, but I did overhear a part of their conversation before I made my presence known. They were talking about moving money between countries; that's all I heard before I felt so embarrassed and guilty spying on my husband, I slammed the front door (which I'd left ajar) and walked straight in.

Phillip jumped up, and for the first time I saw a look on his face that I was to become so very familiar with: furtive. He introduced me to his visitor, and this was the first time I met Max. No surname, although I understand it's unpronounceable anyway. I rather liked him, actually. He seemed charming, gallant in some old fashioned way. He kissed my hand, called me Madame Andrea. He was a big block of a man; laughed loud, long and frequently, but when he turned serious he looked like he was about to pull out a gun. See what I mean about signs; how clear does it have to be that a man who veers dangerously between light and dark is someone to avoid? Max was a package of violence waiting to unwrap itself, but joyful while he waited. He was always ready, believe me.

After that, I conveniently forgot all about Max – and see what I mean? That's so typical, isn't it? Ruffle no feathers, cling on tight, turn the marriage into a life raft.

Phillip seemed happy enough; our finances had improved and we were still at it like rabbits, but I wasn't getting pregnant, which I think we both wanted. I went to the doctor and they did the tests: I was fine. Phillip wouldn't go for his tests. Refused to discuss it, got so angry I didn't recognise him. The sex stopped right then, he moved into the second bedroom and we never slept together again.

When it stopped, the role sex played in our relationship became all too clear. Suddenly, I felt like I'd stepped back from our marriage, far enough back that I could see things for what they really were, without the blinkers I put on every time Phillip's pants came off. I started noticing things for the first time, or perhaps it was just that I couldn't kid myself any longer. Everything seemed rather seedy, but worse than that was the realisation that I'd always known, and lied to myself, over and over.

I began to follow Phillip's political work more critically, saw how the chance to run for councillor started to turn his head. He talked less about the glorious visions of his youth, more about synergies between Labour and business, crap like that. He gained this weird glazed look in public, shaking hands with people you could swear he didn't actually see, or care to notice.

Phillip no longer had friends, just stepping stones to be used appropriately. He started to give political gifts. I heard about this from a friend – you know what they say, my love; the wife's always the last to know? He had money evidently, money I knew nothing about, because it certainly wasn't going through our joint account. He got a new car. I didn't ask – avoiding the issue again – but I remembered Max, thought about that meeting. Said nothing of course: head in sand. You know, it's strange to think we convince ourselves that nothing is going to happen; if we simply ignore all the signs, it will all go away and won't affect our lives. *As if.*

Phillip told me once, I think because he was feeling a bit guilty, he had discovered something important about politics – that to get anything done, you had to 'swim with the tide'. That's exactly how he put it. *Swim with the tide.* Living with him was like watching Dorian Grey's portrait changing in slow motion before your very eyes, a horrid slo-mo video with no rewind button but several fast forwards.

I kept catching shifty looks. He became glib, facile, evasive. Always seemed to have a cover story ready; word perfect, terribly sincere. I went with him to a few meetings, went to a few more on my own without him knowing, standing up the back where he wouldn't spot me. His fire had gone out. It was replaced with some cruel parody of my husband, some sly creature whose patter was oiled to perfection. I didn't believe a word he said because I knew him so well, saw the fiction so clearly. The people though – they loved him, him and his promises to do whatever it was they wanted, his clever way of saying yes without the word actually passing his lips, so he couldn't be held responsible later. Deniability, isn't that what they call it? Fucking hell, he was good at that, the shit.

Mind you, no matter how good he was at it, he couldn't deny the fact that I'd caught him in our bed, his cock half way up some tart. I came home from work, for the last time as it turned out because that was the day they made me redundant. I heard the two of them from the hall, the tart screaming and panting in a strangely robotic way. Faking it, in other words. Absolutely obvious, which begs the question: how is it men are fooled by this? Just how stupid can men make themselves be, exactly, in order to get off?

I was in two minds, standing there at the bottom of the stairs. I looked around at my home, all the mementoes and pictures; the cushions I'd sewn with such love; the dining table all neatly laid out with the cutlery we'd found; the bits of furniture Phillip and I discovered walking hand in hand through markets and antique fairs; the dried flowers and the wedding photos lining the mantle over the Victorian fireplace, the same fireplace I spent an entire weekend restoring, on my knees for hours painting every iron flower and pattern; the drapes my mother made for us; and for the briefest moment I thought about turning round and leaving quietly, so quietly I could come back later and pretend it never happened. I couldn't do it though. This was probably the most important decision I ever made, I'm sure of it.

Step by step, I climbed the stairs. I felt as if I were paralysed, immobile, yet moving on an escalator I couldn't get off, carrying me towards something terrible. The pit of my stomach was hollow with fear. At the top of the stairs I heard Phillip saying exactly the same dirty things to her that he said to me, word for word, another fucking script he'd memorised. I felt sick. I knew that if I just opened the door I'd see them in action. I couldn't bear the thought, so I actually knocked hard, three raps *on my own bedroom door!*

All sounds from beyond the door stopped. I opened the door and walked in. To my utter surprise (and theirs, I think) I found I had absolutely nothing to say to either of them. I just picked up my jewellery box, got my coat and left. I came back the next morning when I knew Phillip had gone to work and collected the other things I wanted to keep. I could smell the whore in every room I went.

Like I said before, I'm no victim; I still feel like I made the choice rather than succumb to the inevitable. Except that all working girls are victims of circumstance, one way or another. There isn't a young girl who has ever said 'mummy, I'd like to be a prostitute when I grow up,' is there?

The worst victims are the sex-slaves – illegals living in fear of their lives all the time – young girls who get brought in by the Russian mafia, by Eastern European, Indonesian or Chinese gangs. These girls are slaves, plain and simple; if they weren't being used for sex it would be something else – cleaning hotels for bugger all, or working as indentured maids. My best friend – Ivy Cheng – she was one, a maid to some Japanese couple who beat her all the time, treated her terribly. She was brought over from Hong Kong, promised a good life and a nice job, but for a price she didn't understand and had no chance to pay off once she got here.

If it wasn't for Dan – he's her husband, or was: she died and it was very sad – Dan rescued Ivy, paid off the debt and married her. Never seen a man so dedicated, so much in love, so completely smitten, as Dan was with Ivy. To my shame, I once tried to seduce him, just to test quite how faithful he really was. He just smiled, lifted my hand off his leg and talked about boxing.

I felt really embarrassed, and still do when I think of it, especially considering how good Ivy was to me – both of them, actually.

I met Ivy at a hostess club – I worked there four nights before they realised I couldn't hold my drink, nor keep from picking up each glass at it was filled. I thought that was what I was supposed to do – get through the booze as fast as possible, but it turned out only the punters were supposed to get drunk. Three nights in a row, I passed out half-way through the evening. Like I said, I like a drink, but not in excess. Truth is, my love – I can't handle it.

This was the lowest point of my life, but if I was honest, I have to admit it toughened me up real fast. Not very pleasant, but probably necessary. I was staying in this vile room in the London Hotel. It's been pulled down now, thank God. It stood just behind the Elephant and Castle, a grim hulk of a place like a tower block, each room a cubicle so small you wondered how they got the bed in. The walls were covered in mock panelling made of thin brown plywood and cheap, unvarnished mouldings. The carpets were stained and ragged and I cannot tell you how much I hated using the bathroom I shared with 10 other rooms.

I talked to some of the cleaners, mostly Filipinos who spoke a little English, and their work was always timed, apparently. Each room had to be done in six minutes in order to meet their quota. One missed room from the quota at the end of a shift and the whole day's wages were docked. Two rooms missed in a week and you were fired. How could they ever expect the rooms to be kept nice when the maids were put under that kind of pressure? It was just slavery, believe me.

I spent several weeks in that hotel room, scouring the papers for a job. My money – what I'd taken from the joint account that first day – was running out fast. I used to eat every night across the road at the pizza place – that's gone now too, which is a shame – and I got talking to the chef, a really nice bloke called Pepi, who looked like a dangerous Sicilian hood but was really a sweetheart. (He's a taxi driver now).

Pepi told me about the hostess club, not recommending it, but telling me a rather filthy story while he twirled his magnificent moustache and leered in a strangely inoffensive way. But he was the one who put the idea in my head, and when I rang up I got a job straight away. Of course it all went horribly wrong, and on the fourth night, after they sacked me, I burst into tears in the back room. The other girls were with customers, all except Ivy. She sat with me, comforted me, made me tea (I feel disloyal saying it, but the tea was vile), and I poured my heart out to her, told her everything.

At the end of the night – I was still pretty drunk and hadn't managed to stand up yet – at the end Ivy bundled me into her cab and took me back to her place. Dan was nice as pie, quite unruffled as he carried me upstairs, put me on the bed in the spare room and closed the door. I stayed there for six months, and I came to love them dearly because when I most needed a home and the security of it, that's what they gave me. Never asked for a penny, never put any pressure on me to get a job or move out, and needless to say Dan never made any kind of advances – there I go, feeling ashamed again.

When Ivy was home we all drank the tea (Dan told me he had 'learned to love' the tea because Ivy made it for him). When she was at work, Dan and I drank strong coffee and modest amounts of cheap brandy, and he showed me fight videos while explaining the finer points to me, like why two grown men were hitting each other, that kind of thing.

One night, Dan took me out to a casino in the west end – with Ivy's permission, I should add. Her encouragement, in fact: they both thought I needed to brighten up, and since Dan had to go to this place anyway he took me along.

I got all dressed up – it was pretty posh – and it was fun. Like a big party with an edge, booze and money and sex. Drugs too, of course, but not openly. (In the girls room, if you breathed in too deeply you'd get a buzz from the coke dust just floating around in the air). Watching big plays was really exciting, seeing huge amounts of money come and go, mostly in the direction of the house.

After a while, Dan introduced me to someone he knew, a floor manager called Pete Grippa, who offered me a job as a hostess, but strictly kosher as he put it – meet and greet, get a drink for high rollers on occasion, decorate the tables, make people feel at home, welcome, that kind of thing. Well, I'd done all that for Phillip, just on a smaller scale, so why not this? I talked it over with Dan and Ivy and they just said 'give it a go, nothing to lose, gets you out of the house', and other sensible stuff like that.

I had a great time. Loved it – dressing up every night. I *do* know how to dress my love, believe me. Great job, playing the gracious host, but without having to worry about paying for the booze or cleaning up afterwards. I swanned around feeling elegant, making small talk, sipping champagne at the tables while I frittered away the chips punters would give me from time to time. *And* I got paid for it!

I tried to pay Ivy and Dan some rent, you know. Neither would let me, but in the end Ivy asked me how much I was offering. I named an amount I thought was fair, and Ivy nodded. 'OK, you give the money to the church' she told me, and that was how it was: every week I popped in to our local church and put the rent money in the collection box. Never missed a payment; I'm proud of that.

The inevitable happened as I guess it must, being inevitable. I'd been flirting all night with a rather handsome Arab, and he asked if I would go to his hotel with him. 'I'm sure a thousand would not be an insult,' he said, sliding a load of chips across the table. Like assuming I'm a whore isn't insult enough. I was just astonished, rendered speechless. The nerve! The effrontery! *The money!!*

Dear God, what a huge amount just sitting there in front of me. I fancied the guy anyway, believe me. And if I was shocked, what happened next was even more astounding. He completely misinterpreted my reaction. He stammered, stared at his winnings and pushed another thousand over to me. 'I'm s...s...sorry,' he said. He really did stammer, and I think he blushed although it's a bit hard to tell with Arabs. 'I didn't mean to offend you. I value beauty such as yours, of course I do'. He seemed quite concerned I wouldn't think him cheap. *Two grand?* OK, I'm convinced.

We had a ball that night, and he became my first customer. My first regular, the best kind. And there it is: how Andrea became Salubrious Sally, a working girl. Circumstance, not victimhood. I *chose* to continue, to do it again, and I have to tell you that any doubts are hard to maintain when you can make several thousand pounds from one afternoon's encounter with a couple of rich, horny Arabs in a two-up. (That was fun my love, believe me. Shocking wanton behaviour, utterly shameless...and I loved every minute. Goodness me, I'm in the right job and no mistake).

My clients were usually nice, sometimes rather unhygienic frankly, but any girl will dump the client straight in a bubble bath in that situation. Some were a bit rough too, but not violent so much as careless, or curiously inexperienced. Soon, I was an entry in quite a few black books, and I didn't need to work at the casino any more, or impose myself on Ivy and Dan. I got a place of my own, my little house, and I did it up really nicely. I wanted it to be salubrious, a little home from home, somewhere I could live *and* entertain. It's how I described my little nest, and that's how I got my nickname. You know, I was proud of myself back then, standing on my own two feet at last – when I wasn't on my back, that is.

Then one day I got a call. I never advertise; too common for words. Recommendation is best, because whoever's doing the recommending won't send me someone unreliable in case it comes back on them. This particular call though – it made me jump. It was Gary Givens. Thoughts about Phillip came flooding back – I'd pretty much put him out of my mind after the divorce and the meagre settlement – and I didn't know what to say to Givens, but I sure as hell knew I didn't want to have him in my bed and I think I made that pretty clear.

He wasn't bothered in the slightest: he just wanted to talk, he said. Just talk. Nothing to do with Phillip – he had a business proposition for me. He was insistent but not unpleasant, and in the end I said yes, I would talk to him, but not here, not in my home. I'd meet him in a pub off the Walworth Road, a quiet place. A public place, just to be on the safe side. What did I have to lose?

When I got there, Givens had already arrived and was sitting alone in one corner with two drinks on the table. I sat down in the empty pub, all mock-Tudor dark stained panels and fake beams, red plastic-covered banquettes, badly painted heraldic symbols on the walls and the smell of yesterday's beer. It was quiet, hushed; Givens explained in a low voice what he wanted. I sat there in silence, sipping my drink as he told me about his wife, Kelly, and the escort agency she ran.

Gary informed me in a sly, boastful way that Kelly had some really important clients but not the right kind of girls to send to them. He made a point about how much money – five grand a turn he said – they were worth, how the clients were all entirely above board and so on, and how his wife Kelly needed a class act on board at her agency to service them – that's how he put it – service them. Apparently, I was to get the impression that I would be the star of the stable; the class act Kelly didn't have.

This all should have seemed very flattering except that coming from Givens it just sounded sordid. I really wanted to turn him down but somehow I ended up agreeing to a trial run. I'd be a liar if I said that five grand didn't play some part. Gary was pleased. 'You'll get on well with this chap,' he insisted as we left. 'Really nice, older man. I'm sure you'll like him, and it will be worth your while, really worth it. Kelly will call you to make the arrangements.

Sure enough, next day I got the call. Kelly sounded hard, brassy – no surprises there. Two things did surprise me: the first was that Kelly was going to come too – this client wanted two girls, so she reckoned. 'You don't have a problem working with another woman, do you?' she asked. There was something insinuating about the question I didn't much like. I'd done several parties by then and didn't mind going both ways. I just preferred the real thing because I could think of better things to do with vegetables, and strap-ons just made me giggle.

There was, however, one advantage – it's always safer when there's two of you, especially when you're meeting a punter for the first time. So I said yes. The other surprise was that Kelly had the impression I'd agreed to entertain in my home, while Gary had specifically led me to believe this would be five-star hotel work. And still the warning bells didn't sound. Or I just didn't hear them.

On the day, I was looking out the window when there was a knock on the back door. I opened it and my mind went completely blank. The punter was standing there, Kelly just behind him. It was Max. As he took my hand and kissed it, I felt a rage inside me so strong I was actually afraid of what I might do, because I recognised Kelly straight away. The last time I'd seen her was in *my* fucking bed, screwing *my* worthless husband.

I have no idea how I kept it together. I think I was helped by Kelly, who never batted an eyelash, just tottered in on her stilettos, took my hand and told me how nice it was to meet me, like we were total strangers. I didn't believe for a minute that she didn't recognise me. She was prepared, knew who I was: Max told me later he had fancied me that first night we met, and when Givens told him what I did for a living after I left Phillip, he insisted that Givens make the arrangement for him. She knew, and came anyway, the brass-necked cunt.

As I calmed down – the rage turning into something colder – things progressed in an orderly way; drinks, small talk, Kelly and I feeling each other up to turn on the old man. I had a laptop and turned it on to play a bit of porn. I'm absolutely useless with computers, my love. Useless. The laptop had a camera in the lid and I turned it on, just to be on the safe side. It never recorded anything though, which is typical. My fault, I 'm sure, but in the circumstances it would have been a godsend if it had captured what happened next. If nothing else, it would help me understand because I can't remember a single thing, believe me.

We were all part undressed, drinking Bolly that Max brought and snorting some coke supplied by Kelly. Max was kind, gentle, courteous even, although he didn't seem very interested in Kelly, who was useless when we put on a little show. Someone once said to me about her fake tits that it was a novel use of concrete. My hand nearly bounced off one tit, they were so rubbery. My skin crept when she started making the same porno noises I heard in my house that day.

She didn't really do anything sexy with me; kept running her hands around like little rodents, never stopping to actually touch, or make contact. Nervous nibbling instead of smooth sensuality. She pretended to go down on me, but she was like a stupid cat – just kept licking my pubes - her tongue never getting near any actual flesh down there. As fake as her tits: all show, no action, as if everything she knew about sex came from watching a really bad porn film while blind drunk.

When Max had seen enough, he came over to me and got on. Kelly sat and watched. I think he regretted Kelly being there, as I did, but even so, I was starting to enjoy this, Max gently rogering like the gent he was, keeping the weight off on his arms (the old ones usually flatten you) and me thinking about how to get revenge on the whore across the room, finding my hatred of her increasing my pleasure as I thrust back against Max.

Then things started getting blurry. The realisation came fast – I was drugged. I was already too far gone to struggle, and Max was still banging away regardless. Then I passed out. Just like that, like a switch: stone cold, out to lunch. It is the last thing I remember.

The official story of what happened is this. After I passed out, Max started to beat me, because that's how he liked to get off. Kelly had also passed out – Max having drugged us both in the champagne – but the story goes that I came to after a while, with Max on top of me still thumping away. I found a knife conveniently within reach – it belonged to Max, a gift from Givens that very day – and stabbed him between the ribs, straight into his heart. Then I passed out again. This is according to the prosecution reconstruction.

I do not remember any of this at all, except for one thing – for a moment I surfaced while I was still lying on the floor. I couldn't breathe because of the dead weight of Max, who was still on top of me. There were many people in the room, bright flashes – police no doubt – then I passed out again.

Next time I came round, I was in hospital with that slimeball Solly Spang whispering constantly in my ear. He represented me at the trial. The deal was this: first class defence brief, no expense spared, and reconstructive surgery for my face at a top private clinic, all paid for by a mysterious third party, in return for a plea of voluntary manslaughter and no mention of my ex-husband or our marriage in any way, shape or form. The prosecution would be brought under my maiden name, which Spang had already given to the police.

Even in the state I was, I understood – Phillip's prostitute wife mixed up with a murder would sink his career if it ever got in the papers. It didn't feel right to me, but I felt so weak that morning, so fragile and terrified, I agreed. I also agreed to forget that Kelly Givens was ever there. I didn't care much about her, nor wonder why Spang wanted to keep her involvement quiet. I still had a revenge to plot, but that had to wait.

I got off, sort of – suspended sentence. Considering it was a manslaughter charge, there was very little of it in the papers, although with me entering a guilty plea and the photos of the state I was in after Max beat me, the judge didn't spend long deliberating.

But strings were pulled, I'm sure of that. There are so many things about it all that don't seem right, and I remain absolutely sure I didn't kill Max. However, I'm not going to bore you. Every time I go on about it, I sound like a guilty whore trying to come up with a new excuse, a new conspiracy theory, a new way of protesting her innocence. I have my theories but I'll keep them to myself.

It's behind me now, and I'm moving on. I'm slowly picking up new clients, since most of the old ones were scared off. Can't say I blame them. *Moving on?* Who am I kidding. What I've told you is the official version given at my trial. The unofficial version doesn't end there, I'm afraid.

Do you believe in coincidences? All the coincidences in my life have been shit. After the trial, I was very upset and quite rattled. I had kept away from Ivy because I'd heard she'd got a job in the council works department, and Phillip was now her boss. This made me feel betrayed in some stupid way, but I got over it in the end, visited Ivy and Dan and we drank some tea. Phillip was never mentioned, nor the job.

After a while, Ivy took me by the arm, just like she did that first night, said 'you need something better than tea' and propelled me forcefully through the door, up the street and into the church. She introduced me to Roger, the vicar and we sat and talked for ages. He was so kind, thoughtful and discrete. Never really asked any questions, just said supportive things about approaching the future with hope, with self-belief, to refuse to be a victim. He was singing my song, wasn't he?

I went to church regularly after that, and that's where Ivy introduced me to a strange young man from Poland called Viktor. Apart from his hair, which looked like he'd caught it in an overhead fan, he was a nice looking boy; skinny and pale, but alert and interested. To cut a long story short, we got on well, and after a couple of meetings – coffee one time, burger another – I invited him home and seduced him.

My God! He was so fit – you wouldn't believe…well, yes…never mind. It was all innocent fun, and we had a nice time. Afterwards, we sat in bed, talking, eating biscuits and drinking coffee, and he told me he'd heard a strange story about me. Didn't ask directly, just sat there with big eyes and crumbs on his chest. I didn't mind – it's one of those things you get used to – so I started telling him the official version. He laughed when I told him about the laptop, how I bungled the webcam. He knew about computers, he told me, and he seemed quite sympathetic.

It was the strangest thing, watching the transformation. He was solicitous, listened without interrupting and nodded in sympathy from time to time. Then, as I got to the part about the old man beating me up, he jumped out of bed in a flash. 'NO NO NO' he kept shouting. 'This is not Max'.

I froze; hadn't mentioned any names at this point.

'How do you know that, know his name?' I demanded, instantly suspicious. Viktor wouldn't tell me, just sat across the room on a chair, naked and defenceless, his legs drawn up with his arms wrapped around them, rocking slightly. He looked really distraught and I felt awful, although I had no idea why either of us felt bad. He just seemed so hurt, so lost. My heart went out to him and I wanted to hug him, but he slapped my face and I backed away, suddenly quite frightened. All he did was dress quickly and walk out. He never said another word. I didn't follow him downstairs, which is unfortunate, because he stole my fucking laptop on the way out.

Agrippa

I saw that turd Pete Grippa the other morning. Enjoying the leather in my new Merc – I do love that 'new' smell – I was crawling up the Walworth Road when I spotted him outside Barclays. He looked as bad as the Walworth Road; run down, grim and scruffy, well past its sell-by date, no pride or purpose. Just hanging on for dear life, for one more chance to stitch up punters who have the misfortune to live there, but not the guts to get their arses somewhere more salubrious. (I love that word – reminds me of a tart called Sally I was fond of – suited her perfectly since she was class brass: Sally Salubrious).

And let me tell you something. I don't care how much money they spend up the Elephant, nothing short of the A-bomb will ever sort out this shit-hole. Mind you, Grippa seemed right at home, know what I mean?

All the shops in the Walworth Road are cramped and over-crowded, like the brains of the people who buy the crap they sell (I won't hear a word against M&S mind you, still good gear even if the gaff is far too small to take seriously). The only people doing proper business are the market, the slot machine parlours, the bookies, McDonalds, KFC and the pubs. Oh, and the Carphone Warehouse – packed all day long with kids, as far as I can make out. Stupid name, considering they don't actually sell car-phones. Who does?

I do like the library up by Manor Place mark you, nice playful little Victorian pile like a fancy wedding cake, never seems quite as grubby as everything that surrounds it. Used to go there when I was a kid because I had a mate on the Pullens estate, a no-hoper musician who made more from dealing coke than playing 'is bass and put all the profits straight up his conk, needless to say. Nice bloke though – completely untrustworthy but when he was on form he was a right laugh, could rabbit at a million miles an hour when he was off his face, but sometimes he still made sense despite having more snow falling from his nose than winter on Kilimanjaro.

Actually a good muso too – saw him in the Green Man down Blackheath once and I was really surprised because he played brilliant, right live wire he was. Guess his career followed his nose...right down the Swannee, as my old dad would say and, like all coke-heads, his habits got the better of his talents.

He's one reason I've never dabbled in gear – I like a line as much as the next bloke, especially since it gets me going in me dotage without the aggro of carting a stiffie around for 12 hours after a bit of the Niagara. I hate that chemical crap; a wrap of charlie that isn't all laxative and sugar never hurt anyone, nor do a few puffs. That said, I wouldn't touch the business end of that little game with yours, especially now the Ruskies have stolen the show from the afros on the smoke front, and don't even get me started about the Columbians. Quick route to the toaster and it's nought but brown bread, mixing with that bunch. Which brings me back to that tosser Grippa.

OK...hang on a mo. I can hear your Guardian-reading fairies grinding their teeth from here. Look mate: I have nothing against blacks (and I don't have a daughter either, in case you're waiting for me to peel off that old chestnut). There's good and bad everywhere and the colour of your skin ain't in it.

But culture counts. The Paks and the Indians have lived here long enough to understand what being British is about, respect certain traditions if you know what I mean, but the Africans – that's a different story. What the fuck kind of country is Africa anyway, when they still believe in witch doctors and mumbo jumbo even when they live in our council flats, have mobiles and flat-screen TV and a nice hand-out from the sosh every week? And the Yardies – even worst! Christ, you can't even understand what they're saying half the time, innit? Patois, they call it, and there was me thinking that was a nice line in paving for the back garden. (Yeah, I know...just my little joke).

I went to Jamaica once, hated it. Belize was nice though, dropped in on a cruise with Dan and Ivy – and Kelly of course, before the trouble – three days we stayed . That's when the thing between me and Ivy kicked off. She was worth it though – best blow-job I ever had – and probably the most expensive too, one way and another. Dan got over it, eventually. (Kelly never did, like I give a fuck). Lovely funeral too, half the borough turned out for that one, but there was more than a few not unhappy to see her pass, I reckon.

Anyway, the blacks are foreigners in a way the paks aren't. No black blokes on the South African cricket team, is there? Indians though – fuck me, they can beat us at our own fucking game, and don't get me started on the West Indies – what on earth happened there, eh? No African tennis players neither, and there's a good reason for that, trust me on that one. (Course, yer African *can* dole out a kicking, so they make reasonable football players even if they do speak frog).

Can't trust foreigners, so I stick with my own. Mostly I think the BNP are a bunch of fascist cunts, which is exactly what my old dad used to say about that vain poof Moseley, but they do have a point on immigration, what with all the Muslins coming in now. I always thought Muslins were Arabs, but it turns out they are afros, pakis, Indians, Romanians, Turks, Indonesians – Christ, they're everywhere!

Nothing against them though; my dad wouldn't stomach it, and neither do I; it'd be stupid really, since I do business with the lot of 'em – every race, creed and colour you can name. (My old man used to tell us how he fought alongside the four by twos in Cable Street back before the war, rather ignoring the fact we all knew he was about five when it happened. Historical events always enlisted him after the dust had settled, like his national service starting just as the war ended, but he didn't like to admit he was just a spectator on the fringes of his own life half the time).

Obviously I can't say too much about my business interests, but I trust you – don't ever give me a reason not to, eh? Let's just say I'm in construction mainly, and the Elephant development is the best thing that's ever happened to me, even if I do have to deal with little shits on the Labour council, people like Phillip Goodfornothing.

Trouble with people like him is the backhander isn't what they really want – not that they have any trouble trousering the loose change mind you – they also want to further some bollocks political agenda *as well*. That's what they want the money for half the time, not just for themselves like normal people. I guess they convince themselves it's OK because the money's for the greater good (like Marx ever did dick for me, right?) but we can all play the self-justification game, can't we?

So it's grease for the slippery pole rather than bubbly on a yacht or a villa in Puerto Banus, and I won't mention where that pole gets rammed up half the time, just tell you this: never bend over the table in the voting booth. I'm not kidding. Ambition ain't in it, believe me; lust more like. A man who wants money can be trusted – within limits – to do what's required to get it. A man greedy for power can only be relied on to stitch you up once he has it. If hypocrisy was radioactive, the town hall would glow in the fucking dark and we could save a fortune in street lighting.

Don't worry. I'm getting there – just painting in a bit of colour, that's all. Background colour, isn't that what they call it? I'm telling you all this stuff because I want to make you understand the difference between my line of business, and the kind of shite a twat like Pete Grippa gets up to.

Not to be indiscrete about it, my profit from the supply side alone on the Elephant construction, let alone the labour, has a fucking lot of zeros on the end, know what I mean? Grippa's childish crap is lucky to break three zeros on a good day. Peanuts for monkeys, right enough. Like corner shops, small action for pennies made from scratching off sell-by dates, while Tescos have to open their own fucking bank. (I'm Tescos, in case I haven't made the point clear enough, although I haven't quite got me own bank yet...but hey! Give me time, Lord. Give me time).

Grippa's operation – if you could call it that – was about as kosher as his old man's back street garage, all black tarry stuff and filler in the sills, exhaust bandages, dodgy MOTs and Evo-Stick retreads, with a bit of Radweld in the radiator to stop the leaks just long enough for the punter to make it home, but not back again when they figure out what a mug they've been. All that for a couple of ponies profit. What the fuck way is that to use up your life, constantly stitching up punters for bugger all? Him and his dad got the crap beat out of them on more than one occasion, and quite right too if you ask me; and because it was a street-side caper – well visible – the old bill were forever on their case as well. A bad case of JFO, as we call it round here. Just Fucking 'Opeless.

One time, when he wouldn't let go of something or other like a rabid dog with lock-jaw, I made a joke. I said 'we ought to call you Agrippa from now on.' Twat looked at me with a totally blank face. Not a glimmer: probably thinks the Romans are in the Champions League, that's how much he knows. I'm talking about Pete Grippa, you follow?

My point is this: he has the IQ of a doughnut; a ring of stodge with a fucking great hole in the middle. I never liked him from the start – did something that really pisses me off – called me Gibbons instead of Givens. More monkey business. I've had legs broken for calling me that, not that I'm touchy or anything, just can't stand that kind of disrespect. Never show any weakness and never apologise, that's what my old man used to say and he was spot on about that, if little else.

Ah, sorry...I'm wandering again, ain't I? Half Brahms now and my glass ain't refilling itself. Your round, I believe?

Cheers. Right then – you want to know about me and Grippa, right? It's like this: one time I had this prospect. Back then, I was flush from...well, never mind what...but I always liked the fight game and I happened to meet Roger Dodger – he's the parish vicar, really nice bloke, dead genuine but not preachy or holier than thou, just down to earth and wants to do good, the mug. No, I don't mean that; lots to be admired in someone who cares enough to be that dedicated. Just hard to believe at first, always trying to figure out what his game was, but after a few years we all come to realise he actually meant it. Rare breed, sure, but don't knock it.

Anyway, I see him somewhere or other and he tells me he got this kid in his club down Kennington Lane who can do the business, so I drop in and take a look. It's an Asian boy called Ali, and he's hard as nails. Toothy grin, outsize feet like a puppy but with a wicked delivery that could floor you in one.

So I have a chat with the boy and Roger gives me the idea of managing him, which I quite fancy. Then I bump into a veteran cut-man – that's Dan, who I mentioned earlier – and two and two just add up, if you know what I mean. Dan suggests we need somewhere to train so I cop the lease on Patrick's old place, a bit run down but in an area I think will come under the cosh soon, so it's a reasonable investment no matter what, since the resale will be worth more than a few bob. (I was wrong on that one as it turned out, but never mind. Or fifteen years too early, depending on which way you look at it).

Off we go then, and bugger me if Ali just can't stop winning. Points mostly – just a few KOs here and there, but everybody sees he's an up and comer and the dosh starts rolling in – prize money on the one hand, good returns on the side-stakes as well. I'm really enjoying myself, pleased when I see Roger the Vic I can look him right in the eye. Straight business, no funny stuff at all. No, really – don't look at me like that. No capers, no dodgy dealings or monkey business. Quite proud of meself I was, I can tell you. So was my old man.

Thing is though, money talks the loudest. In the end, it shouts down everything else. I was grafting like a mad bastard, but I couldn't get a look in on the top end of the card. All locked up by the likes of Mickey Duff and the emerging Frank Warren (Jack Solomons was long gone by then and that twat Hearn was still in short trousers). They wanted such a large slice of the pie, there was only crumbs left for everyone else. I had to come up with a plan B, if you follow me.

I know what you're thinking, but don't be too hasty to sit in judgement. It was like this: I couldn't take the boy any further by the look of it, not without getting into a lot of aggro and investing such a lot of time and money it started to look like an attempt to climb Everest in me underpants without a Sherpa.

I told Ali at the time, I said: 'Look son, sometimes you have to take a view, as the bankers say...' (that's not rhyming slang either – not in this case) '...you have to take a view of yer career, invest in the future. Everyone does it if they have sense. So just go with me on this one and I'll take care of you. After, I'll release you from your contract so you can sign up with these people, top people, and they'll see you right'. I meant it too, I really did – more or less. Dan didn't like it much, neither did Ali, but both could see the sense in what I was saying so that was that. Or should've been.

Ah, cheers. God I want a fag; this fucking ban is bollocks, ain't it? Labour twats. Sorry – as I was saying, Plan B was simple enough. While I was flogging the dead horse trying to get a decent fight for Ali, one of the big boys – I won't mention who if you don't mind – expressed an interest in acquiring his contract. The more I thought about it, the more sense it made, because there was a good deal to be had on a quality prospect, maybe a percentage on future earnings, and some cash up front with a bit of luck.

All I wanted – no word of a lie, mate – all I wanted was one decent fight so I could stand in the ring with my boy and feel the love, hold his hand up in the air like the champ I was sure he'd be one day – just not with me as manager. It was a simple fact of life really – I was a bit bored with the fight game anyway by then and other grass was looking greener, if you take my meaning. One last payday and time to retire gracefully from the fight game, hang up the old gloves.

The argy-bargy over the contract didn't actually take long, although there was a good reason for that as it happens. They did make me a really handsome offer, percentage on his future winnings and everything, and I thought I understood why they were so keen to point out the deal depended on Ali's next performance – justify their investment to the board and the press, all that jazz. (If you can see this coming, you're a better man than I was then, but the way it turned out that ain't saying much, so don't get cocky).

Anyway, we did the deal and, good as their word, they lined up a cracker of a fight at Bethnal Green herself, fourth on the card of a unified middleweight belt decider. Blimey, I thought: THE BIG TIME. Don't look surprised – I don't mind admitting I was young once too. Haven't always been this shrewd and neither have you, so fuck off with your grin. Your round, and do leave off with the bleedin' ice. What am I, a fucking Eskimo? Neat if you please and a bag of their best scratchings wouldn't go amiss.

Cheers. So I told a few people, as you do, and a fair few bob went down on Ali, who started at 25-1 against and went into the ring at 11-4. I was very confident. So was Ali. Dan was quiet though, frowning all the time and complaining. A right worrier, which led to the misunderstanding that followed, me blaming him for what happened (and I suppose I did overreact a bit if I'm being honest). Of course, I know now that he's always like that, always has been. Doom and gloom, which is odd in a corner-man because they are supposed to gee up their boys.

Dan came at it a different way, trying to make them cautious while working them like dogs so on the night the engine would purr smooth and powerful, like my big Merc driving right up Sally's tunnel. He always said 'if you over-estimate your opponent, the worst that can happen is you get a nice surprise. Other way round and you'll likely take a thrashing.' Spot on; voice of experience if ever I heard it.

I won't bore you with the details of the fight, just say this: having taken the first five rounds without breaking a sweat, half way through Ali looked tired. Never seen him shagged out that fast, and he'd been the distance three times in the last five.

In round seven, he was moving at half speed and getting tagged with only his reflexes saving him. I was watching from the back, so nervous I thought I was going to need rubber pants any minute. I could see Dan and some young kid he'd recruited as a towel man, both of them bollocking and encouraging Ali. From where I was, at the end of the seventh I thought he was going to fall off the stool any minute. He looked like some pensioner who needed a quick nap.

In round eight he could barely raise his arms. The crowd were booing now, 'cos all Ali could manage was to cling to his opponent— an excellent Scotch with a cunning line in below the belt business – and so was born the moniker 'armtwister' due to the way he was hanging on like a drunken dancer. Towards the end he actually looked like he was pissed and by now I was smelling the proverbial rat, so when he went down for the count I didn't head for the ring, but out the door in a fucking fury the like of which I haven't felt before or since. If anyone had crossed me at that moment I swear I would have topped them on the spot.

I couldn't think straight, had no idea where I was going. It was pissing down with rain and I got soaked, ending up somewhere in Shadwell before I came to my senses and caught a cab home. Oh – one other thing then. The towel man Dan had recruited? You'll never guess who it was?

Next morning I found Dan at home, still trying to swim to shore after drowning his sorrows. He had no idea where Ali was, or what had happened to him. All I could get out of him was that Ali could barely speak after the fight, and didn't seem to know what fucking day it was, let alone why he was dripping claret all over the dressing room. I went to my little office down the Camberwell end of the Walworth Road and sure enough, there were several messages from the promoter on the machine. I didn't fancy talking on the dog so I went round instead.

They were nice as pie – several people there all expecting me, apparently (a show of force, I realised later, in case I got stroppy) and they all shook their heads together in puzzlement like Thunderbirds puppets on one set of strings, apologetic and disappointed, but the gist was this: the deal was off. No discussion, no negotiation, just lots of head shaking and mealy-mouthed concern. The contract was cancelled with a finality that reminded me of every meeting I've ever had with my bank manager, who definitely is a banker.

'Hey, Pepi – over here mate. Be with you in a mo...'

That's my taxi, so I have to love you and leave you. You look puzzled – like I've done the patter but not pulled out the rabbit. Well, here it is. I find out a few weeks later that they signed Ali anyway, cut me out completely. I complained to the Board – not that they give a shit – and the bastards just blanked me, said I had signed a document freeing Ali from his contract (which I had, but

I thought it was cancelled along with my deal) but of course they didn't mention *that* when they produced a copy and waved it about like a flag of surrender – my fucking surrender, right?

So you put two and two together, don't you? They want the fighter, but don't want to pay anything for him. What devalues a fighter most? *Losing*. All they needed to do was fix it so Ali would fuck up. But how, since neither Dan, me or Ali would have bought it?

I mentioned Sally early on, and I owe her one for this. She had a mate on the game who told her she'd done a party, got saddled with, or should I say saddled by, some idiot who couldn't stop talking about hisself. Full of it, apparently, and took forever to stand up, he was so off his 'ead. There they were (eventually) bonking away, and even as he's pushing the plunger he's rabbiting on about how he fixed some fight, *how he doped the fighter to slow him down.*

'How could he do something like that?' asks cunning Sally, her radar going full tilt. 'Oh, he said he was in the corner, or somefink like that. I wasn't really listening,' goes the tart. 'Who was he?' says Sally. The tart looks puzzled for a minute, then her face brightens. 'Can't remember his name, but he kept saying how he was a pirate. No...wait...I've got it – Pirate Pete. That was it.'

Case closed, and the start of a long, cruel wait for me. My taxi driver, Pepi – he's Sicilian – he'll tell you the value of the long wait, but it was worth it in the end...sorry, but that's one for another time. I'll just say this: I haven't finished with the cunt yet, not by a long chalk. I'm off mate, and thanks for the tipple you tight git, seeing as how I'm still waiting on me scratchings.

Pepi's pizza

Hey. How you do, mate? Your door ain't closed proper – sure, that's it. Ok, where you wanna go? Oh really? I know that address. You going to see Fahrenheit Freddy, right? I know him, sure. Too well, maybe. He's OK now, I think. I know what you think. You think, why Fahrenheit, right? Sure, no big mystery, just little joke. Is because Freddy want to be called Freddy Mercury - before Queen, see - but he don get nowhere in showbiz. Then big gob bum-bandit come along and name is taken from then on. We think - mercury, thermo...thermo...mommy...anyway, Fahrenheit. Geddit? You know how long it take Pepi to learn how to say Fahrenheit? Fuck, I hate English and you crazy words, right up till somebody tell me, they say: 'Pepi...' (is me, Pepi) '...Pepi, Fahrenheit is not English word, is German.' German, should have known. Bad tippers, Germans, I tell you straight. Fucking foreigners.

Basta! Where your fucking 'ell plates, eh? Idiot!

Sorry 'bout that. You see what he do - cut me up like that. Hey, sure...good idea, put on a seat belt. Why not? Oh look, look! You see that, eh? You see that place, there by bus-stop? That's where we make the pizza, in that hole over there. Before hole, sure. You like pizza? I make a fantastico pizza, Sicilian style, you love it – dough light and crisp, thick base, not mean thin thing like stupid Italians in north – no good pizza in two hundred klicks from Milano, no kidding. Crunchy bottom but soft too because of thickness, this is Sicilian secret – OK, not secret really, but you know what I mean. Use only the best ingredients, we ship in from Italy mostly. It was good place, super oven, all shelves same heat. Very important, this; we make two hundred pizza a night, right? All come out exact same. Anywhere in oven. Exact. *Ai!* You know what? I just remember. Fucking oven was German.

I see you before, right? In pub with mister Givens. I drive for him all the time, regular. He ask for Pepi always, which is good because sometimes he pays me for whole night, most time I spend sitting in cab reading while he...he visit his friends. Yes. And tips after. Tips very important in my business, you know. Hey, don need to tell you this, eh? I can see you are generous person for sure, right?

How you know Freddy, huh? No, sorry...not good I ask this. You don't answer, OK. How about I tell you how I know Freddy, much better. I meet him at restaurant, see. He come in regular, sometime takeaway, sometime sits at table. Seems like nice person at first, gets to know us. Help us too when we put on little show downstairs – more tables down there but we don use at beginning 'cos not enough people come. Later, we get very busy when people hear of Pepi's amazing pizza, and we open downstairs too. Now we think, how about music, something nice? Freddy helps us, gets us microphone and speakers and stuff, good too – no rubbish, 'cos Freddy knows about this. He eat with staff sometimes and also he play downstairs I think. Sure, definite. Don remember much about music though, too busy in kitchen.

Then later, when they pull down restaurant, we don find another place so no work, and all good Italian places in town don want my pizza, so I drive cab instead. They don like Sicilians and we don like them neither. Calabria OK, it is south like Sicily. Basilicata and Puglia not bad, but Campania all stupid farmers and Napoli is not so good place, no good at all. My wife, she's there now, stays with her mother. And my son, Guido, he's there too with wife. Well, ex-wife really. Great little boy, my Guido; big belly, loves his food and his papa. I miss him, sure. One day...*basta*! I dream too much, pass house. Sorry. I back up.

There you go. Here is Freddy's place. Thirty six pound please...hey – just my little joke! I fool around, alright. I know you, know you not stupid tourist. Six pound fifty, tip up to you.

Life Below Decks

I was brought up to be a musician. My parents were very single-minded about this; from the moment I displayed an ability to hum a nursery rhyme, I was deemed *talented*. No escape from my genetic destiny. No inadequacy could undermine my parent's belief in this talent; equally, nothing I did could ever fulfil it. In their eyes, I was perpetually delinquent, and lived with their contempt and disappointment until the day I moved out. Man, is this a heavy burden of expectation to lay on a child.

Looking back, it seems strange that my parents spent so much time trying to extinguish every last flicker of fun from playing music. They had working class sensibilities, all scales and arpeggios; the musical equivalent of a numeracy drill, rote learning obedience and military rigour. They didn't sacrifice time and money so I could have fun; I had to work, and look like it.

The joy of it: I still remember as an infant what fun I had, what exuberance I released by pressing those black and white keys. This enjoyment, once displayed, was systematically suppressed in favour of duty, of practice without aim or purpose. Since there was no pleasure at the end of it, no reward, to a kid this is pretty pointless. Strange too they missed the best trick of all: I have always been very competitive, and gregarious. To have entered me for competitions would have been the perfect strategy, the perfect incentive. Instead, I just got really bored with the whole thing.

You can't blame me for becoming resentful. I can't blame my parents for making me that way either. I tell myself they did their best. Lucky for me, while they succeeded in making *their* music dull as dishwater, I found some of my own and it was anything but dull. Nothing they did could put out the fire, it turns out, and nothing was more incendiary than playing very loud and very fast. Rock and roll, man. *Rock and fucking roll!* Probably saved my life.

Things came to a head when I was fourteen, a year when five momentous things occurred: I got laid; bought my first two albums – both Hendrix; learned a Thelonius Monk piece; joined a band. *And refused to have any more piano lessons.* My parents shook their heads, sighed, and disowned me in all except name. I had disavowed my calling, choosing instead to play trash and therefore to *be* trash, to have no future, none at all. Since this was the point of rock and roll – 'hope I die before I get old' – their attitude rather cheered me up, as did the fact they were finally off my back.

But if my folks did manage to instil one thing, it was ambition. You can only be told you are talented so many times before you come to believe it, and create expectations to match. I had some seriously wide horizons. Trouble was, I didn't really have the talent or the skills to fly me first class to the pinnacle of my choice. While my head was in some lofty place, the rest of me would be playing Tie A Yellow Fucking Ribbon in a working men's club in Peckham. Neon lights. Concrete floors. Formica tables. Stale smoke. Threadbare carpets. Cheap beer. A handful of indifferent people, half cut.

Only one solution: drugs. Yes, I know...cop out, all the usual guff. Thing is, it made the music bearable. Blitzed, even some twonk singing Little Green Apples in a key not known to man nor dog can be a manageable kind of pain.

Don't be too harsh. It's a job, right – but with a difference. Every night, I would go somewhere to do violence to the thing I loved most. I longed to be Keith Emerson playing convoluted mock-classical concertos; the reality was northern cabaret clubs playing bad Tamla Motown covers. I wanted to be grinding out relentless, hard sexy soul; ended up in a tiny German bier keller basement off Oxford Street in a cheesy band fronted by a mad trombone-playing scientologist. I wanted to be a punk: I did six months playing Girl From Ipanema on the boats to old ladies trying to cop a feel every time you walked by. ('Ooh, *young man!*')

After a few years of that, you realise something, the reality hits you, and hits you hard: you are going to spend your *whole life* below decks, jammed in with the rest of humanity. The upper decks, the jet set sunshine and deckchairs – they were out of bounds, the province of the successful, the accomplished, the captains of my industry. You don't even *see* the stars from below deck, let alone dance among them.

When you realise this, when you know for sure and can't kid yourself any longer that you're really going to make it if only you can hold on long enough…believe me when I tell you that a joint may be the only thing between you and losing it. I stood at the rail some nights watching the dark water pass by. It looked inviting. Especially when you have ambition the size of the Empire State, but only enough ability to fill your cabin locker, and that with room to spare for some slippers, a change of pants and two good books.

Look. Nothing I can say will *not* sound like I'm making excuses, so I'll say no more, except this: I'm out of the business – dealing – have been for some time. Strange thing is, I just got busted for something completely unrelated. I was burgled, and local junkies stole my instruments. I'd just returned in a cab and when I found the door smashed in, I freaked completely. A neighbour came out and told me she'd seen two kids running with guitars, heading into the Heygate estate – a right dump, believe me. Pepi – the taxi driver that brought you here – he was still outside, so I jumped in and we caught up with one of them.

What happened next is really baffling to me. I'm completely non-violent. Completely a pacifist. Wouldn't hurt the proverbial fly. But that day I went *completely* mental. It was only Pepi dragging me off the kid that saved his life. He was badly beaten, unconscious. Pepi grabbed me, I grabbed the guitar. We jumped back in the cab and Pepi drove me home. I thought I'd got away with it, but somebody shopped me – not Pepi, I'm sure of it.

Somebody else. Somebody who knows the thieves. Somebody I had run across before, or run over; someone you've already met.

Gary Givens.

These blocks are called the Pullens Estate, or the Pullens Buildings, depends on how old the residents are. Out front were another two blocks, but they pulled them down. Nice gardens now, sure – but at a price. Over a hundred flats gone, and since the remaining flats are selling for more than quarter of a million quid a pop now, I think we can assume there was nowt wrong with the ones they pulled down, since they were identical and all built at the same time. Typical council thinking – if you could call it that. Still, a bit of greenery does cheer the place up, for sure.

The baths down at Manor place don't exist anymore either, not as such, although the building is still there; council offices now, where smarmy bastards like Councillor Goodhall work. You know about our Councillor Goodfornothing and his Shit-Works committee? Right job for him if you ask me, since he's a piece of work himself, and always has been. We went to the same school just round the corner.

Gravy Givens was also there for a bit, but he got booted out like he did from every school he ever went to, right little thug that he was. Typical bully, just a long streak of piss for a backbone and more front than Harrods when it came to lying through his teeth (surprising he didn't go into politics like Goodhall, now I think of it). He used to kick the crap out of me, right up until I twigged I'd grown a foot to his three inches and now looked him in the eye, a point I made clear one day when I blacked it for him in the playground and he ran off crying like a baby. I think Givens still hates me for that, and I'm sure he was the one who shopped me, but what goes round comes around, as they do say.

Here you go – one sugar, right? I dunno if you're interested in local history, but my family goes back a long way on the Pullens

– right back to 1922 – although the estate had already existed half a century before that. A local firm, James Pullen and Son, built it and my mum told me she remembered a Mrs. Pullen working in the estate office, so I guess it remained in their hands right up until the council got hold of it in 1972.

Amazing enterprise really, typical Victorians; they put up 700 flats in six tenements – this was started in 1870, the year Dickens died – each block had four stories, and the whole lot was built out of London Stock bricks, really lovely, although you wouldn't think so considering how dirty they get. Better kept now since the money moved in, but that fucked the community yet again. Keeps happening, a sense of community builds up, and then some outside force, always motivated by money, comes along and buggers it up.

This was an estate built specifically for the working class, remember – tenement buildings and little two-storey workshops arranged in yards down the centre of each block. I don't know for sure, but perhaps working class families were encouraged to start ventures of their own, because the workshops originally had a door through to the flat behind it. The rents were certainly modest, but for its time I reckon the facilities must have seemed luxurious to the working class people moving there.

At one end of the estate, they built the Manor Place baths, which had a fair-sized swimming pool that was always freezing cold. They used to put boards down over the pool and have dos there, and for quite a while it was a well-known boxing venue. I saw my first fight there, caught the bug if you like. I went regularly, so inevitably I would see Givens from time to time. He always scowled at me.

Next to the baths, there was a wash-house with baths, showers, laundry tubs and wringers, and all of it was built specifically for the use of the tenants. It's grade 2 listed now, which I think is nice. What else was there...let me think? Well, there was the primary school I went to, a few shops and the management offices, but of course the main feature was the workshops. They did an amazing range of stuff, for sure – stationers and printers; the acid smell of ink and the regular mechanical clinking and slow breathing of the platen presses is an echo from my childhood I can still hear right now.

There was a company that made ship's fans, a hatters, bookbinders, a feminist HQ for some radical agenda (although nobody could find out what it was – early days, I guess), a place that made paint brushes, furniture and carpentry workshops – I can still hear the abrasive metallic singing of the saw bench in my head. One firm, J&J Lilleycrop, they were the official furniture restorers to the Inns of Court. There's an anarchist bookshop now, quite famous and still going – 49, I think it's called.

But the best – the one I always remember – was the Industrial Clog-makers. How brilliant is that? They made them for the Fire Brigade, apparently...no, don't ask. I have no bloody idea. Are clogs slow to catch fire? Mind you, thankfully there was one thing that wasn't allowed, and that was car repairs. Only one firm ever set up shop there and they didn't last very long at all, what with being run by Sid Grippa and his son, know what I mean?

Christ, it used to be so nice. But things change; it's the way of things for sure. There was a time when the Pullens became very run down, because the council realised that if they cleared the land, it would bring them in a fortune compared to the tiny fixed council rents. They had their eyes on the development opportunity and the huge amount of loot that would bring in, not that much would make it to the council coffers mind you. Backhanders galore, always has been. And favouritism, which is where the connection between Goodhall and Givens crops up, because Givens was after the demolition contract. In fact he was after rather more than that, it turned out. Oh man, this is getting heavy. Listen, you look like you've been around, know the world. I can roll up a nifty little sharpener if you like? Up to you?

Shit yeah...DAMN! This is good weed. Right on, man!

Oh, do fuck off – I'm pulling your leg. *The colours! The colours!* Calm down, it's just a joint. I sometimes wonder how much dope I got through in the Pullens, how many tons. There was a vast amount of it around because of the travellers and squatters – no hard stuff at all, as I recall, just a lot of smoke and a few pills, maybe a bit of speed – I guess I'm trying to say that heroin didn't figure, which is just as well. I'm talking about the mid-seventies, the age of squatting really, and I tell you what: the squatters saved the estate.

You remember I said about how the council wanted to pull it down? Well, in the run-up to that – over quite a few years – when a flat was vacated, they just boarded it up and wouldn't rent it out any more. Apparently, they had consulted this solicitor, Solly Spang, a local specialist on evictions who did a lot of work for Givens (what kind, I shudder to imagine, frankly). It was he and Givens who came up with the idea of the development in the first place, and when the council – or more likely Goodhall – couldn't think of a way to get the tenants out, they just started boarding up flats one by one, playing a waiting game.

The estate looked sick, diseased almost. It was really horrible, like the place was waiting to die. Lots of bad drugs around then – junkies in the stair-wells all the time. But then something drastic happened: the squatters got wind of the situation. The word went out – they were well organised in those days, considering there was no internet – and in a matter of a year every vacant flat seemed to be occupied, all the boarding gone, and the life came back to the place. With a vengeance actually.

And the thing is – and the papers or the council will never admit it – the thing is, they were brill tenants. They fixed things up, painted the outsides, they organised and opened shops that had been empty for years. They started all kinds of alternative businesses in the empty workshops, and they formed a really strong Resident's Association which took on the council to stop them demolishing the place. And you know what, man – we only won, didn't we. It was fucking far out, actually. Damn, I fancy a bit of pizza. You hungry at all?

I love all this history stuff. If you ever go to the Pullens, take a look at where the wall meets the pavement. There's a concrete ledge raised six inches off the pavement and projects a foot from the wall, and you'll see all these regularly spaced flat metal disks all the way along. They are all that's left, the stubs of iron railings that used to run along the front of all the blocks. Very decorative I guess, but they were hacked off at the base and melted down during the second world war.

Another thing – in my first flat on the estate, when I took over my grandma's place, there was this big crack in the front room wall that nothing could fill permanently, and it was caused by a doodlebug, a V1 that landed just up the street. Funny the things you remember. They used to call it the parlour, my parents and grandparents. In fact, they never used it after my mum got married (I'm talking about the maternal side of my family) so it always seemed musty and airless, which it was. The smell of dust and old polish.

But it had a huge upright player piano in there, with loads of piano rolls stored under the green-velvet covered lid of the piano stool, all transcriptions of classical pieces. I used to sit in there for hours, pedalling like mad as fast as my little legs would go, watching the paper scrolls and their strange punch codes unwind their mysterious messages, decoded into glorious (if rather mechanical) music through a wonderful Heath-Robinson arrangement of pipes, bellows, knobs, levers and keys.

Oh man, that takes me back – my first memory as a human being is from the Pullens, standing in the ground-floor well at the back between a pair of flats, always dark and foreboding, looking upwards through a towering, brick-defined rectangle, staring at the bright sky a long way away. I was two. Hey – I've got some superb 70% Fairtrade plain chocolate. Fancy a bit?

I often wonder how much we are shaped as kids by seemingly unconnected incidents. Talking about the player piano reminds me of my granddad. He was an amazing bloke – I never heard anyone ever say anything about him that wasn't a variant of 'what a nice man'. He was a truck driver, worked at the docks most of his life. He fought in the trenches in first world war but never spoke of it, not to me, anyway (he died when I was thirteen, so we never had a chance to talk about adult aspects of his life, which I really regret).

He was a pipe major in the London Irish and he still had his pipes when I was a kid, although weirdly my mum can't remember ever hearing him play them. He played the ukulele too and did a fair 'Leaning on the lamppost'. I'm sure he knew loads of risqué songs too, he was that kind of bloke – cheeky, irreverent but never disrespectful. I can only remember feeling joy and love in his presence.

He was patriotic though and not anti-war; he used to give me and my brother books full of photos from World War one; I have a monochrome image of Canadians fighting in a forest that has never faded from my memory. We used to go on trips to the war museum – the Imperial, just up the road – and I loved every minute, the highlight of which was climbing into the cockpit of an Avro-Lancaster (just the cockpit, cut off like the head of some great beast, because the museum is small and couldn't get any more of the plane inside); another permanent memory like a snapshot. Not a thought so much as a picture taken by a small boy standing in awe far below the strange Perspex- bulge of the cockpit and forward gun turret, but with nothing behind it. I loved all the knobs, dials and levers, just like the player piano only a lot bigger.

And just like a church organ and its pipes and stops and more bellows, bigger and faster, lots of wheels and levers working like mad. My granddad – his name was Bert – he worked during my childhood as the handy-man stroke caretaker - this is after he gave up driving trucks – at that weird Seventh Day Adventist church in Regents Street that looks from the outside like a cinema. He used to take us there occasionally, my brother and I. That's where I got to play the organ and peer at the innards. (I played the organ again for the first time in a long time at a funeral recently – a woman I knew called Ivy, although I did have mixed feelings about doing it. Playing that organ brought back memories, I can tell you).

My point is this: what did these experiences do to me, what effect did they have? My love of music and years of playing, my interest in military history, my love of machines and electronics that led me into audio engineering and computers? I even learned how to fly. I would love my grandfather even more than I already do if any of these abiding interests were in some way his legacy. They were a wonderful gift.

Jeezus I'm blitzed. Listen to me, foaming at the mouth. Hope I'm not boring you. Have a crisp – they're sea salt and black pepper. Wanna split a beer?

Back to the story then, for sure. Sorry about this.

The squatters: as the place filled up, there were a few abortive attempts at eviction, but the squatters were well prepared and knew the law. They banded together when the bailiffs turned up, got the police and the media around straight away, and after a few tries the council gave that up and changed tack.

They had finished building a new estate of nice little houses and two storey flats all along the northern edge of the Pullens, and they offered them to the occupants of two blocks between here and Manor place. The tenants accepted gladly since the new places were much nicer, and next thing we knew, the bulldozers moved in. We were powerless to stop them. It took a year of hell and dust and unbelievable racket, but at the end, two blocks and the street between them – Thrush Street – were gone. And every so often I would see Givens, sitting in his Merc, watching the huge wrecking balls tear through flat after flat, home after home. It was the blitz all over again.

We were all stunned, and in some cases deafened, but we were never defeated. The council had plans to start building on the cleared site, but unfortunately for them, a band of travellers we tipped off turned up and occupied it first. It was an invasion, and there were loads of them all over the place. It was great. Each summer for several years we had an annual festival; many times I supplied the electricity for the stage by way of ten plug boards all connected in a line, the whole thing suspended from a lamp post and raised up three floors and through the window of my flat.

All during this time, it's curious how little effort the council put into getting the travellers off the site. They refused to meet the Residents Association. They appeared to be doing nothing at all. What did happen was rather more sinister and covert. People started coming home to find their flats smashed up. There were quite a few muggings all of a sudden. A workshop was firebombed, although the thing didn't go off, luckily. Cars were stolen – a DC I know told me more cars were disappearing from our estate than all the others on his beat put together.

One evening, three men knocked on a door, forced their way in and beat the tenant, his wife and a friend who was visiting. Windows were smashed in. There were a surprising number of busts. I was freaked, as were quite a few of the long-term tenants, but the squatters and the travellers had seen all this before. The travellers especially had a few right hard cases running with them, some even having hardware, it was said, although I never saw any.

These people – alternatives – are brilliant networkers, as we call it these days. When you sell dope, you get to know lots of people, go lots of places. You're welcomed, not because they like you but because you have what they want. They get high with you, and when they do they start gabbing away, especially when charlie is involved. You learn things, hear things, and as ever, intelligence is valuable, especially when it's pooled. The alternatives are very good at pooling their resources; smart, cynical, realists not hippies, and they know the system better than the people who run it.

Gradually, we built up a picture of what was happening in our manor. People were seen in pubs, and connected to events on the estate. Crims like a smoke or a toot, and heavy hints were dropped while collecting or getting fired up. Travellers are also traders by nature, good at a bit of barter, so they often found themselves in possession of information acquired along with consumer goods needing a new home, doing business with people who preferred anonymity and never took cheques.

And every bent alley, every back street and devious turn, every roundabout and crazy-paved path – they all led one crooked way, like drunken roads to Rome. They all led to Givens.

I lost sight of him for a while after I left school, what with all the travelling around. The story goes that he started off putting the squeeze on a few Pakistani shop keepers who had family members upstairs they didn't want known about. He ran a little extortion racket on local car dealers, supplying them with fake MOTs, then demanding a rake off to stay quiet. Next he moved into the pubs, forcing them to buy booze he was bringing in from France, and one pub who wouldn't go along suffered a fire that gutted the place.

He owned several workshops where cars went in blue and came out red. And we kept hearing about ugly stuff, how he fancied himself as Joe Pesci's character in Goodfellas (or was it Casino?) There's a story that he put some bloke's arm in a vice once. Another time, he broke a man's leg with an iron bar for calling him Gibbons instead of Givens.

But the worst stories were about his properties. He had flats in New Cross, Camberwell, Peckham – had the rent-books on quite a few council properties, apparently, taken from frightened immigrants who he forcibly moved elsewhere, or just scared off. He was reputed to tell new tenants in no uncertain terms what would happen to them if they fell behind even a week on their rents, and many came home one night to find all their possessions dumped on the pavement, the doors locked and barred, or a new family installed and cowering behind the windows as the previous tenants picked up whatever wasn't smashed and twisted by Givens' boot boys.

But we had no proof, nothing we could use. And this is where I come into the story. I was only on the fringes of the Association, although I knew everyone well enough. I knew what was going on, but didn't want to get involved – not in the line of business I was in. At that time, aside from dealing, I was working six nights a week in a small combo, playing standards in a hostess club. It was full of incredibly drunk Japanese business men who spent fortunes on whisky and vodka, getting hammered and singing very strange songs we could never accompany.

The girls were mostly on the game, would go back to a hotel with clients who were too drunk to do much when they got there, but there was one who just smiled and nodded and poured the drinks as fast as she could – the girls make their money as a cut from how much booze they can pour down their customer's necks – and this was Ivy, the woman whose funeral I played at.

She was a lovely little thing, quiet and discrete, always had a smile and a knowing look about her. Oddly enough, she was Chinese, which you'd think the Japs would hate, but they seemed to like her and were always trying to get her to go with them back to the hotel. She never did: one night as she was leaving, a little corporate type was waiting for her outside, unable to get a taxi. He spots her getting in to her pre-booked cab, and tries to commandeer her and the cab.

I came out just as this happened, and saw Ivy trying to get out, panic on her face. She broke free, ran towards me with the man following, the driver half out of the car and immobile. I'm not brave but this was a little bloke and very drunk, so I put out my arm to stop him. He does a quick impression of a pissed martial artist, I tweak his nose for him and he falls back down the steps. For a moment I was a bit worried, but he sat up, rubbed his head, vomited and walked off.

Ivy was shaken, so I took her home and saw her safely inside. Nothing much was said, she didn't ask me in, just offered a shy 'thank you' and that was that. What changed though was her attitude to me. Where before she had been polite but remote, now she was chatty. Just with me, not the others, and only when we were alone, sitting quietly on rainy nights when nobody came to the club.

Sometimes she told me about her childhood in Hong Kong, or about living in London in the early days, when foreigners were distrusted automatically. How she'd found Christianity, helped by our Roger Dodger – he was the new vicar back then – and what a comfort she found in the church early on, when she was all alone. It sounded very sad, although there wasn't a trace of self-pity about her. And one night, quite casually, she told me about her other job, her day job in the Southwark works department as a clerk.

For Phillip Goodhall.

The others wanted me to exploit the relationship when I told them. Some suggested that her association with the hostess club could be used to blackmail her, an idea I hated and refused to discuss, which is pretty ironic for reasons I won't go into. The decision was mine, and I decided just to mention the situation to her at work, dead casual, just to see what happened. One night I did just that. Told her that I lived on the Pullens, about the council and Givens, the harassment and the violence. She said nothing, just smiled grimly and poured more tea. That was it. No reaction at all and it was never mentioned again.

About a week later, there was a knock at the door. I opened it to find this lovely policewoman on the doorstep. She was very polite, making sure I knew straight off that she knew about me but she wasn't here to bust me. I invited her in, and had the strangest conversation of my life.

Her name, she said, was Marty Bannermann. *Marty!* No old bill had ever offered their first name before. She was interested in the activities of 'a certain Mr. Givens' (police do talk funny sometimes, like they're in an Ealing film). Said she wanted to help me at the same time as furthering her investigation which was, she told me with theatrical confidentiality, unofficial.

This immediately made me very suspicious. I guess she saw that, because she launched straight away into an interesting story. Apparently, she'd been on the up at the Serious Fraud Office, good prospects and all, when she came across information that led her to a certain councillor. *And then she got sacked!* That's how she put it. I asked if she was no longer a policewoman, but she showed me her warrant card, explaining she was effectively demoted.

The implication was obvious; Goodhall has got her removed, although Bannermann wouldn't name him, which I thought was completely ridiculous. It was obvious from the way she'd told the story – no other way you could understand it really – but she couldn't bring himself to actually say the name, so we talked in code.

Deciphering it, the message was that there were questions about property, questions about money dealing, questions about connections with firms getting all the plum contracts, and one in particular. Too many questions, all connected to Goodhall in some way.

What Bannermann suggested next actually shocked me, coming from a police officer (sheltered life, me). What, she asked, would 'someone' do to prevent these questions being asked in the press – if somebody threatened to leak the story, for example? *What would somebody choose to do about the fate of the estate, in order to keep their name out of the papers?*

There it was; a lever to stick up Goodhall's arse, courtesy of the old bill. It was up to us to work out how to use it, but the threat of exposure would bother a greasy politico like Goodhall no end.

Then the invoice arrived. It was a trade for information: Bannermann wanted everything we had, what we knew, had found out, seen or heard - everything about Givens and Goodhall, and any connections. Anything. All the people connected with Givens. Sites he was working. Deals he made or pies he had a finger in.

The way she put it, it was obvious she knew we'd been collecting this information, and then I remembered my conversation with Ivy. Did she know Bannermann? It occurred to me that I had said much too much to the quiet, smiling little lady fussing over her tea. There are some people you just pour your heart out to. No wonder she made the best tips of all the girls. Damn, she was a real good listener, for sure. Easy to underestimate, as I found out.

I discussed the deal with the others. They were deeply suspicious, but I pointed out that Bannermann had acted in good faith, delivering her part of the bargain before we had even agreed to deliver ours. There was a lot of hot talk about collaboration and the Nazis – don't ask me why, but they always crop up in the traveller's arguments.

Eventually, the others caved in (I supplied some lethal Jamaican bush, which may have had something to do with it) so I gathered everything we had, wrote it up – a useful exercise in itself – and met Bannermann on Southwark bridge one night to hand it over. I had a surprise for her, too, although I had no idea how big until I saw her face light up.

It was an invoice from some blandly named company, made out to the works department, stamped paid and with a cheque number written inside the imprint. It arrived – and this is the weird bit – in the post, a couple of days before I was due to meet her on the bridge. Across the top was scrawled a single word: 'Banaman'.

To this day, I have no idea who sent it, what it was or what it meant, but I think it made Bannermann very happy indeed, for sure. Of course, since Ivy worked in the council works department, I did wonder, but I knew better than to ask. In fairness to her memory, I should tell you that she never gave me the slightest sign she knew anything about it, not even a hint. I kept a copy, by the way, just in case.

We got a bit carried away, I think. It was decided that the best way to tell Goodhall what we knew – even though we had no proof of course – was to call him. By now, we also knew about the Russians – came across them a few times and one of them rather naughtily gave us a couple of titbits about demolition jobs that were interesting.

So we got Annie, actually a Romanian – which we reckoned sounded Russian enough to fool Goodhall – to make the call. We made a party out of it, a load of us gathered in a big converted Bedford truck turned motor home. It was hard not to giggle, listening to her while she just kept repeating 'SFO, Mr. Goodhall…Serious *Fraud* Office investigating you…SFO. Nobody know this…yet. Stop trouble on Pullens and nobody ever know'. After the third repeat, she hung up.

We all looked at each other, a bit surprised and, in truth, probably a bit scared. But nothing happened, the bus wasn't stormed by SAS, bombs didn't go off and…well…it was something of an anti-climax really. We all got completely ripped and eventually went to bed.

We knew of course that the sign we'd been successful would be no sign, no trouble. The absence of evidence, if you like. But we got a sign the very next night. Two workshops were firebombed and this time the bombs went off. The little free press outfit burned to the ground, and the whole-food shop we had set up was gutted, all the stock ruined.

We got the message. We decided – by unanimous vote – that it was time to deliver ours. The next day, we met a journo we knew from the local rag, and we gave him the lot. It didn't take him long to get a quote from the SFO, and they ran the story two days later. The day after that, the nationals picked it up.

We thought Goodhall was finished, politically as well as with the council. How wrong we were. They did deselect him – he was angling to be an MP – but he kept his job and was re-elected councillor later on *as well*. But a new planning application had gone in (we were watching for this) and it covered the entire estate, so we had achieved absolutely fuck all except to severely embarrass Goodhall.

We only had one card left to play, and I was the one to suggest it. I had my copy of the invoice I gave to Bannermann, so another copy was made. We couldn't find out much except that the company was owned by Givens. We assumed, correctly as it turned out, that the invoice in some way connected him with Goodhall, probably through the cheque number, because this would allow someone like Bannermann to track where the money went. The copy was delivered to Goodhall's house one night, with a typed note that just said, 'give us our estate and leave us alone. This isn't the only copy'. We figured that although we didn't know the significance of the invoice, Goodhall certainly did.

And we were right. Two weeks later, a new plan was floated in the council chambers. It turned out that the council was completely strapped, and they had to withdraw the previous plan they had submitted because they couldn't afford to execute it. Instead, they said – and this was cute – they had to do something with the site to prevent it from being overrun by undesirables (that's the travellers of course), so they would turn the whole thing into ornamental gardens; walkways, trees, benches, play area – the lot. For the good of the residents, they said. For the residents' use, and to improve the area. Yeah – right!

Still, we saved the day, and our homes from demolition. After that, many more of us bought our homes under the right to buy scheme. By the time the council had enough in the treasury to consider attempting another stunt, we owned more of the block than they did.

I thought that was the end of it, I really did. I had a new job, playing a residency in the Old Kent Road, with another in Blackheath on Saturdays. Both good bands, old pros making a wage. Never ever rehearsed or changed the set, mind you, but the money was steady and I didn't need to anaesthetise myself before I climbed on stage.

One day, there was knock on my door. More policemen, but these were neither polite nor friendly. They arrested me, searched the flat (no gear, luckily) and next thing you know I'm on bail, waiting to go to court on a charge of aggravated assault against the bloke who stole my guitar. Too much of a coincidence, I think you'll agree, although how Givens found out I have no idea. Sometimes I think he never even knew. He was such a git I think he was still getting his own back for the day in the playground when I blacked his eye and made him cry.

For sure.

The Chicken's Progress

This one morning, I was down in the cells with my clerk, seeing a client. He was up for GBH , a right shtarker and guilty as Goebbels. Not my problem; my job isn't to judge, just collect the fee. We get talking; turns out the prison van broke down on the trip down to London. My client hadn't eaten since last night. The minute we walked in he started pleading for food, and it was obvious he wasn't faking it; pale, a bit unsteady, bulging eyes – looked like he was auditioning for a part in Schindler's List.

I'm not soft – far too many villains on my patch for that – but a client in a state is a liability when you put him in the dock. I turned to the clerk, fixed him with a stern stare (he's a flaky little tyke otherwise) and told him to get this man something to eat - anything - but to do it very, very sharpish. We were due to be called any minute and the nearest shop was quite a schlep. Off runs the clerk; I wade through a few finer points with my client – like not picking his nose in the witness box – but I can see he's not paying attention, so we wait. And wait.

Eventually, the clerk runs in with a carrier bag and hands it to the client, who reaches in and pulls out...a chicken! A complete, shrink-wrapped certified kosher roast fucking chicken! Nothing else. 'What on earth...?' I say to the clerk, who shrugs as he watches the client try (and fail) to rip off the shrink-wrap. 'Only thing they had, next store was another ten minutes away.'

I'm about to say something cutting when in marches a bloody court officer. The usher has summoned us, so we all troop upstairs behind the officer right after my client is cuffed to a guard. (The usher isn't a man you keep waiting, nor is this particular judge – any judge, come to that). As the officer reaches for the door into court, I notice out of the corner of my eye that my idiot client has the chicken stuffed under one arm and is still trying to get the wrapping off with his free hand. I grab at the poultry – big bird, like my mother would use to make the soup – and the fool starts a tug of war, as if I'm trying to mug him. I wrest the chicken from him, and clutching the bird – my God, it was heavy – I turn to find the usher staring at us through the open courtroom door. He sees the chicken, then fixes me with a glare I don't ever want to see again in all my life. I panic, dump the chicken on top of the pile of papers in my clerk's arms, and we march into court like that: my client drooling and licking his fingers, never taking his eyes from the chicken as he bumps into every bit of furniture between the door and the dock; my clerk walking behind him in a kind of stately procession as he crosses the courtroom, holding the chicken reverently in front of him on a platter of parchment; and I take my seat at the defence table, trying very hard not to look at the judge or the briefs, both of whom are staring in disbelief at the chicken's progress. A pervasive aroma of roasted chicken, onions (and possibly sage stuffing) follows the clerk across the room.

Eventually I have to look at the bench, and the judge gives me a stare even worse than the usher's. He scowls at the chicken, which is glowing sort of nuclear orange atop the pile of papers, then back to me. 'Well, Mr. Spang', he remarks, in a tone dry enough to mummify the jury on the spot, 'do you intend to enter this poultry in evidence? Call it for the defence? Mr. Usher, swear in the witness if you please.'

No reply required, of course. The jury start laughing, only to be silenced by another glare from the bench. Nobody moves; everybody is staring at the chicken. I swear I could hear several stomachs rumbling. The usher finally breaks the spell, decides not to push his luck – I'm sure he was thinking of some little jest of his own – and approaches the dock to swear in my client who, for the rest of the afternoon, sits gazing at the roasted bird, drooling copiously onto his shirt as he gives his disjointed, and largely contradictory, evidence. Our brief only makes things worse:

carried away with the lofty rhetoric of his obfuscation each time his client says the wrong thing, he leans on the table, but in fact rests his weight languidly on the chicken and promptly slides off, unbalancing him in the middle of his oratory.

It's turning into Carry On Up The Courtroom now. Our client answers all the questions put him in a vague way, staring off to one side of the barrister and towards our table: the only time he took his eyes off the chicken was when they led him back to the cells. As he passes our table, he glances up defiantly at the judge, grabs the chicken, tears a leg right off and walks out, devouring it with Tudor glee. For a minute I was sure he would chuck the bones over his shoulder as he left court. (I think when the judge passed sentence - found guilty, needless to say - he probably added an extra year for that caper. I should worry? I got paid. In advance).

My practice was in the office block half way down the Walworth Road. It's a lively area, full of colour, especially the market. Vibrant, you might say. Not as good as Brixton, but teeming with the salt of the earth. (That's a euphemism for 'potential clients', got that?)

I didn't live there, thank the lord. Got a nice place next block over from Harley Street, corner flat that cost a few bob, I can tell you. And don't get the idea that I spent all my time defending scum, either. Sure, there's a steady income to be made from the low-life, but it's hardly very edifying. Not what my old dad imagined when he named me Solomon, that's a dead cert. No wisdom required. Funny thing: the low life all called me Mr. Spang – forelock-tugging respect ain't in it – but my better clients call me Solly. It's all very Yiddish, but hey – their money isn't. Good gelt like everyone else's. Plenty of it too.

Best thing is that my better clients don't need much reminding when the bill comes due – I know too much for them to take any liberties, not that I'm implying I'd be unprofessional or anything, just that one has to know who one's friends are, and look after them, isn't that right? Anyway, that's all behind me now. Behind me.

The best work is civil, no court appearances or entanglements with the bill. I don't care for them much, to be frank; I've known bent coppers all my life, dealt with them when I was a nipper, drunk with 'em, been to a few of their filthy parties – you have no idea what those boys got up to with porn and drugs from the evidence lock-up, brass blackmailed into performing and turning free tricks in a backroom, an entire squad pissed out of their minds, and at the end of the night, they jump into their cars and drive home.

On my life, this is what they were like back then. Hard men, capable, knew where they could do business and where they never could – able to tell the difference between the professionals and the scumbags. What's the diff? The pros never shot at coppers. It was the just the odd scumbags who went mental when they got caught. The pros in those days understood the limits, even the mad buggers like the Krays or the Richardsons.

Everything's changed, isn't that right? On both sides of the fence. I swear to you that the bill these days are so self-righteous it makes me want to vomit. They really fancy they're doing good, half of them, like fucking social workers. Bureaucratic to a turn; probably got a procedure for wiping their arses. So polite now, so prim and proper. It ain't that they don't bend; there's no barrel of apples ever that didn't have a bad 'un. All you have to do is look and you'll find one, and usually more than that. But they don't take money anymore, not most of them. It's information they want. Knowledge, intelligence – these are the currencies of crime now, get it? Basically, the entire system relies on blackmailing one criminal to catch another.

So it's all pleas, grassing each other up. You know: done for drugs – get off by ratting out a neighbour, a bloke down the pub, your mates. Wives shop spouses just to get rid of them. They've turned the local populace into a criminal Stasi, I swear to you. A gang does a job, then they all turn on each other when the wheels come off. The crims end up hating each other, no more honour between thieves at all – if there ever was, mind you. They look over their shoulders all the time, can't trust even their own mothers, so they tool up, going shopping with a nine-mil auto in their pocket.

Next thing you know, people get shot for littering. Drive-bys. Every drug dealer from here to Newcastle – armed and dangerous. So many drugs around, so many guns; inevitable you end up with so many stoned morons with a mobile in one hand and a piece in the other. Do you know, nearly half the criminal cases I worked got done because of their mobiles? Total morons texting their mates, saying 'I'm on a job, digging into Natwest from the hairdressers' basement. Fancy a beer and a curry after?'

On my life, I swear to you, I've had clients placed at the scene by phone records showing calls going through masts right by the crime scene – one time it was actually on the roof of the jewellers they were doing – at the exact time of the robbery. I heard once – don't know if it's true but sounds about right – that one idiot actually used his moby to take a photo of his mate drilling into a safe. It was still on his phone when they caught him.

When you say to them 'why didn't you leave your mobile at home' they say: 'can't do that, mate. I'd be lost without me moby' or 'I never thought of that'. Morons. The professional criminal class is long gone; it's funny, but a woman the other day mentioned social cohesion. It made me think: as social ties broke down in the area – it was very family oriented before the seventies around the Walworth Road and Old Kent road – as the families moved out or broke up, so did the community.

The criminal community also broke up just the same way, the hierarchy of respect, the firms, territories – the families, to coin the mafia phrase. Crime these days is senseless, the violence obligatory, the ambition petty and no skill is ever required except to point a gun or steal handbags off old ladies.

Oh dear – listen to me. I kid you not, I'm growing senile. I'll be whistling Dixon of Dock Green next and saying 'it's a fair cop guv'. Rose tinted prison overalls. Ignore what I said, except the last bit. The rest is bollocks.

No, fact is I much prefer the contractual work, a little negotiation and some smoothing of paths, you know – a facilitator, let's call it that. Several important businessmen round here are associates of mine, much more than they are clients. A lot of the work is for the council: I do sensitive contracts for the works department, for example, sort things out for them.

Phillip Goodhall, the councillor, he runs it. Influential man, Goodhall. I know him well – although not as well as I thought, to be frank. When I first met him he was on the way up, seemed like, until he had his own run in with the police. One in particular – and I mention this because if you run into her you should know what she's like – her name is Bannermann. DI Martine Bannermann. Mean, vicious type – quite the vindictive bitch; more or less destroyed Mr. Goodhall's reputation, she did. To this day I don't know why, but now Bannermann's at it again, and this time I swear she's after me too.

She's a smart girl, is Marty Bannermann, although some say the smart ones make the worst coppers. Who knows? Thing is, she's got a good head on her shoulders, which is why she ended up in the Serious Fraud Office. Deep thinkers, that lot. Have to be, trying to get ahead of some seriously devious people. Now, at the same time Bannermann was hiking her skirt up, trying to get off the bottom rung of the SFO, Phillip Goodhall was pounding the pavement, angling for the Labour MP nomination to stand against Simon Hughes, reclaim Bermondsey from the orange biscuits.

Goodhall was a popular councillor, apparently. This depends on who you talk to, but in the circles that mattered – Labour party movers and shakers, local business leaders, union shnorrers, town hall execs and civil servants in the know – with these people he made his mark. Every schmuck thought he was a good guy in with a chance. Including me. Oy fucking vey!

Thing is, Phillip was – how can I put it – well, he wasn't hurting, do you see? Nice cars for him and his lovely wife, big house down Kennington Lane – steps up to the portico, pillars, tall windows – and a weekend place out by Braintree, shaggy thatch, beams and Aga style , so I heard. Parties full of chattering classes drinking champers – coke-fuelled orgies, some say. Days at the races for the favoured, all paid for. And contributions to almost anything that moved – lefty political candidates, local charities, boys clubs, help the old gits, battered wives, fund-raisers for people in places you never heard of before, or after – you name it, Phillip was a vociferous advocate and his generosity always seemed to come with a photographer attached and a column in the next day's paper.

Rumours started – inevitable given his profile – but Phillip didn't try to hide anything, or didn't appear to, anyway. He made a statement about his property investments, and they checked out. The papers dropped the story and that appeared to be that. But by coincidence, Marty Bannermann had picked up a trail of some kind at the SFO, a trail that one must assume crossed Goodhall's.

Look – I wouldn't want you to think that I was being disloyal to a client, or breaking any professional confidences, but there *was* something odd: how did Goodhall get the properties he developed? Where did the finance come from? I have no idea, and I'm sure Phillip has a good explanation. I've never asked him – didn't seem proper given our relationship – but I do know that when Bannermann started asking questions about Goodhall's largesse – he'd made a point of being very public about it, after all

– when questions were asked, Phillip was concerned and came to me for advice.

'Sol,' he said to me, 'Sol, I'm afraid that mud will stick at the wrong moment. It doesn't matter who throws it, you know how this works.' Of course I understood immediately. This is a good man, a decent man – this is what I believed back then, I swear to you on my life I did.

The problem was what the politicos call perception – if the news gets out that he is, by some accident or even malicious design, involved in some investigation, and not just any investigation, but one by the SFO, this would sink his chances of selection. It would hang over him like a cloud. By now, most of us thought the nomination was a dead cert, and in a few weeks it was to be confirmed. But the rumours kept circulating like stale smoke. Bannermann was doing her vengeful rain dance and the clouds were forming.

We met several times after that, Goodhall and I. Each time, the topic was the same. He had confirmed that Bannermann was behind the investigation, and the focus was related to money-laundering. I must have looked a bit baffled when he told me this, because Phillip laughed. 'I know, it's ridiculous, isn't it?' he assured me.

'Of course' I said, agreeing with him. Like I said, I don't judge. Then he changed the subject, and told me the legal team on the works department was overloaded, and could I take on some of the overflow contractual stuff. And let me be clear about this: he never suggested any kind of connection between one discussion and the other. Not then, not ever, got that?

Now, if Goodhall were here, he'd tell you that what happened next was my suggestion, but I don't remember it that way at all. *Not at all.* The idea was that if Bannermann was somehow transferred out of the SFO, perhaps the investigation might fold. Along those lines, anyway. We did discuss it, I remember that, but I swear to you on my life I don't remember suggesting such a thing.

A few weeks later, that's exactly what happened. I'm not saying there was a connection, don't get me wrong, but you know the Labour Party headquarters in the Walworth Road? Well, Phillip was up and down those steps like a tart's drawers. It was like one big party in those days, already so popular they thought they could pull off whatever scam Mandelson thought up next with impunity. Point is, Goodhall had friends there, party workers I'd seen at his place. They were backing him for selection, I expect. Next thing you know, Bannermann is transferred. On my life, I have no idea why.

Mind you, the old bill had the last laugh. Somebody – I'm sure this was Bannermann calling in a favour – somebody decided that the best place to post her was Manor Place nick, down the Walworth Road, so now she was breathing down Goodhall's neck again, which hardly pleased Phillip. Bit of an own goal in some respects. According to some, Bannermann was going mental about the transfer too – a demotion, she called it - which explains what happened next.

A story appeared in the local paper, quickly picked up by several nationals. An 'unnamed source' had told the paper about the SFO investigation in which the name of a certain candidate had popped up. No evidence was found, says the paper, and the SFO refused to comment, although they eventually confirmed that the case had been closed, apparently.

That was all, but it was enough. The cloud formed, good and dark, and it pissed down all over Goodhall. After a few days, when it was obvious the story wasn't going away, he was called before the selection committee, who stood by him for all of thirty-five seconds before pulling the plug and nominating someone else.

And that should have been the end of Councillor Goodhall. But not quite: the locals, enraged by what they came to see as a complete stitch up by the police and the local papers, re-elected

Phillip as councillor out of spite, although quite how Goodhall managed to pull that off, nobody knows for sure.

Now I have to be honest with you here. I'm not going to pretend I didn't know that some of my clients' dealings were less than kosher. Take Gary Givens, for example. Good client, known him many years, but he isn't the kind of person you want in your house, around your children, to be frank. I did contract work for him, gave him advice from time to time, sorted out a few of his boys who got themselves in a bit of bother.

Naturally then, I became aware of certain opportunities – investment opportunities – which I wouldn't normally have considered. But times were tight – aren't they always? – and I may have speculated a little without paying too much attention to the background mechanics, do you see?

What I'm saying is this: I had no idea how deep things went, how far Givens was prepared to go, why in some quarters he was called 'Grafty' Givens. And I didn't know how well-connected he was either.

One night I went to a party at Phillip Goodhall's place. It's very nice, you know – plush, tasteful, not at all the kind of place you'd expect a Labour stalwart to wallow in; no working class squalor, no bare boards or rising damp, knotty pine furniture or ethnic lamps. Oh no – it's all Persian rugs and Swarovski crystal, antique bookcases, first editions and objet d'art littered around the place. They had a Hockney, I think. I sound a bit green-tinged, don't I. Maybe I am, because someone in that house had good taste. Me? I don't have the eye or the dosh. But my point is this: what kind of credentials are these? Labour? Left wing? *Socialist*? Don't make me laugh.

I remember I was at the party talking to Ivy Cheng, a woman who worked for Phillip at the municipal works department – she was his secretary, as I recall – when Givens came over, grabbed my arm, and took me into the study.

Phillip was there, but Givens introduced me, not realising Phillip was my client. Odd Phillip never mentioned it to Gary – this was the first time I realised how close he held his cards. Anyway, it turns out they've been working on various projects for years, which I had no idea about, and they want to use my services, on retainer to a company they want me to set up for them. Offshore. The fee they offered was generous, but not outrageous. (If it had been outrageous I would have been suspicious, honest).

That was how it started, casual and straightforward. It just happened that their business expanded and there was more for me to do, so much that in the end I stopped taking on new clients. Most of the work I did for them was in the form of advice, consultancy if you like. Tax law, legal movements of money, property, trade and employment law, import export and transport regs, that kind of thing.

It was inevitable that as they got to know me and trust me, they would be more candid, more direct about their dealings. That's normal, ain't it? But look, what am I supposed to do, eh? Grass up my own clients for what they are thinking? After all, it isn't any different to my other clients in many ways. I often know they're guilty, they tell me as much. I still give them good counsel, represent them to make sure they are treated fairly by the law – that's my job, right?

This was no different: I was giving legal advice to Givens and Goodhall, knowing they were exploring aspects of the law in order to exploit it. No crimes had been committed, just discussed. There's a difference, you know. That kind of advice, how to find the cracks in the system - that's what accountants do, isn't that right? No difference really. Anyway, I don't judge people. Their business practices – none of my concern, to be frank.

That's what I told myself, anyway.

There's plenty of work going on in a borough like Southwark. Lots of developments all the time, commercial and residential. My life, we were busy. Givens and Goodhall worked closely together on many projects, and this generated a lot of work for me, of course. But the big money was on the horizon, and everyone had their eyes on bits of the prize: £3 billion for the Elephant and Castle redevelopment.

Now then...that's real money, I kid you not. Demolition and site clearance alone are real earners, because you can put a load of monkeys on the job, don't need a word of English, just know which end of a sledgehammer to grab. Disposal of the spoil and dangerous waste? If you call a skip full of broken bricks a hazard to health, you can charge twenty times as much to dispose of it, do you see? To the casual observer, it might have appeared like the entire Elephant and Castle complex was built out of asbestos, I kid you not. Let's leave it at that, just to say that it's another area of law I'm expert in, not that it makes much difference what I'm expert in now, by the look of it.

The first sign of trouble came when we picked up Goodhall one night in Given's Merc – the old one, not the one he drives now. This was strange in itself, having a meeting in the car while we drove aimlessly around Camberwell. Givens was furious with Goodhall. A juicy contract had been redirected during the tendering. It had been marked up for us, but ended up going to a company we knew was a front for the Russian mob in South London. Goodhall kept saying 'somebody got at my staff', which was likely true, but Givens remained furious and entirely unforgiving. It was just as well for Phillip that Givens was driving, his hands being occupied, do you see? Eventually he dropped us off, Phillip and I, and drove off again like Sterling fucking Moss, tyres squealing and swerving about all over the road.

Nothing more was said, not in my presence anyway. Then one night, quite late, my phone rang – 2am for fuck's sake. It was Phillip. In a very calm manner he told me he needed my help. I could tell by the strange, flat control in his voice that this was serious? He asked me to meet him somewhere, and I agreed. I didn't ask what it was about. The urgency was enough.

The place where we met and parked our cars, it turns out, was half a mile from where we were going. We walked the rest quickly, in silence. Several times I started to speak, but Goodhall just silenced me with a look. Without warning, he turns into an alley between two rows of small brick new-builds, goes through a gate, up a garden path, and knocks very quietly on the back door.

It opens instantly and we walk in. Kelly Givens closes the door behind us. She's in a business suit, glasses, and she looks...well, she doesn't look like anything, actually. Just blank, vacant. Like a mask, a rigid mask of self-control, like Phillip's voice earlier. I get a chill down my spine, and no wonder. She leads us into the lounge, and there on the floor is a girl, mostly naked, unconscious. She's been badly beaten, and it seemed rather evident that the dead man with a knife in his side lying on top of her had been doing the beating. The room is in disarray, signs of a struggle, stuff knocked over.

'Well?' says Goodhall. 'What's the best course of action?' I have no fucking idea, I kid you not. 'Tell me exactly what happened,' I say to Kelly, who is brushing her hair with a steady hand. 'She killed him in self-defence. It's obvious. Look at her face. He did that, the bastard. What a swine, deserved what he got if you ask me. Fucking animal.'

'What are you doing here?' I demand. 'Is she one of yours?' Kelly runs an escort agency, a good one; reliable girls, no bad drugs. Used it myself from time to time when negotiations required a little sweetening. She nods. 'I booked it. Her first bloody job for me. Poor cow: she hit the panic button that comes through to my phone. I came as quick as I could'.

'You didn't call the police?' I ask, although this is a formality. She gives the correct answer straight off: 'Last time I called them, it took six hours for the car to turn up'. I look at the body, the death-white immobility. I never realised how still a body looked when it was dead. Like something made out of very ugly marble.

'Who is he?'

Kelly shrugs. 'The girls call him Mad Max. He's Polish, I think.'

The girls call him... I file that one away. 'Did he book through you?' I want to know, especially if there are any records in her office. There will also be a record of the call if he used a mobile. Kelly nods, but she seems to be ahead of me. 'No booking note. Call was from a phone box – took it myself.' I don't ask how she knows it was from a phone box. I get the feeling very strongly that I don't want to know anything else at all.

'Does anyone know you're here?' I ask, turning to Goodhall. 'And what about you?' I can't fathom the connection, do you see – or why he'd take such a risk coming here. He could have just sent me, couldn't he? Goodhall glances at Kelly and I suss it immediately. They're at it, which is rather naughty, bearing in mind what a mad dog Givens can be, and suddenly it is clear to me that this has become personal, too: it would mean a very substantial loss of income for me if the business relationship was destroyed, largely by Givens killing Goodhall, Kelly, or both.

This is really not good for business, not good at all. I know it sounds selfish, but it seemed to me right then I had no option but to sort this out to protect *my own* interests, never mind theirs. As practiced as these two were at deception, they still managed to make a right tangled mess of their own fucking web.

'She called me,' is all Phillip says. Kelly nods, then tells me nobody knows where she is, and that – curiously when I look back on it – her car is parked right near ours, half a mile away. *I came as quick as I can.*

'I'm missing a bit of the puzzle here Phillip, and it's time you gave it to me. Why did she call you?' I demand. I'm getting nervous.

Phillip glances at Kelly again. 'She…' he looks at the unconscious girl on the floor – for the first time, I realise – 'she' my ex…my ex-wife'.

For a moment, my mind just went blank; it's still the most unexpected thing a client ever said to me. This isn't some mugging, some aggravated assault; the word 'murder' forces its way into my head, the seriousness of which clears the fog.

Years of experience kick in. I think quickly. 'The best chance we have of keeping the lid on this is if we call the police now, with me here to look after things. That can only happen if somebody has called me, otherwise I can't explain how I came to be here. That would be you Kelly – you called me after you got the panic alarm, asked me to take a look for you. Got that?' Kelly smiles, a grim little tightening of already thin lips.

'Phillip, you have to go very quietly', I tell him, 'very normally, to your car. Go home and stay there. Park your car round the corner from the house instead of on the drive, in case anyone sees you – that way, you can say you were just out for a walk, down the shops or something. Kelly, see if there's something upstairs with a hood that Phillip can wear. Then come back down sharpish, we have a few things to discuss before you leave and I make the call'.

Goodhall agrees. As he zips up a hoodie that Kelly finds, I can see he's thankful for my help. He has the sense not to ask any questions, but a particular look confirms to me that his generosity will be demonstrated later, and in copious quantity, of this I have no doubt. Phillip knows the cost of certain things, and is willing to pay for them. He pulls up the hood and leaves through the back door.

Kelly is upstairs in the bathroom. I sit and look at the grotesque scene on the floor. Very little blood. The girl groans, but then goes quiet. I want to pull the old man off her, cover the girl in a blanket, but I dare not touch anything, disturb any evidence. Kelly comes back in, sober face scrubbed of makeup. She looked old, haggard, and strangely defiant.

We run through the options in a hurry: these days they can time a death pretty accurately and we can't afford to sit around chatting with a stiff lying unreported on the carpet. Doesn't look right somehow, does it? I get the sense that Kelly's watching me, studying me. Spooky, I kid you not. She never looks once at the stiff; I can't *stop* looking at it.

But she doesn't get it, do you see? Doesn't get that *I* get it. 'Kelly, why is your car parked so far away?' I use my interrogation voice, the one I use on clients who are barefaced lying to me. Kelly jumps, the mask slips, and for a moment I thought she was going to cry – that would be a first, I kid you not.

'Never mind' I tell her. 'I don't need to know anything, but I can't protect your interests unless I understand how they might be threatened. The details are unimportant right now. Obviously, your best interests are served if you were never here, but there is a snag, isn't there?' She knows what I'm talking about, acquiescent now.

'It's her, right?' she says.

I agree. 'She is going to need representation. The charge will probably be manslaughter, but they might go for murder, you never know. Either way, if I was appointed her legal representative I would have access to her as soon as she wakes up. I can ensure she doesn't speak to anyone at all until she has her story straight. Only thing is, let's just say she wakes up very confused, thinks you came here, you were here earlier, and doesn't remember using the panic button. When was that installed, by the way, this being her first job?'

I pause theatrically, laying it on like a barrister in court. She knew the score, so it was time to get down to business. 'Look, no need to say anything, Kelly – it's just a hypothetical – but just tell me this: what would it take to set her story straight, do you think, if that were the case?'

'Well, she wouldn't bite the hand that feeds her, would she?' says Kelly. 'Or in this case, the hand that pays the legal fees.'

Good: we understood each other. Kelly will cover my bill – and it will not be small, neither – not a case like this, and now I'm appointed I can control events to some degree. With the business taken care of, Kelly leaves through the back. I call the police. And ask for an ambulance.

The case was pretty straightforward. Why wouldn't it be? Open and shut, clearly. They do talk to neighbours – routine – but nobody saw a damn thing, heard anything. The usual. The girl, Sally – she's a puzzle because after an hour of scene of crime photos, forensics running around dressed in plastic bags, she still hasn't come round. I point out that they really need to get her to hospital before the delay starts looking like incompetence or just plain indifference, so they bundle her into the ambulance and I go with her. Turns out she'd been drugged, GBH so they tell me later, and since she's hardly likely to have drugged herself, the stiff takes the rap. All adds up nicely, assuming you don't know what I know. Needless to say, I kept my thoughts to myself.

When she eventually comes round, Sally can't remember any of it. She remembers the punter arriving and starts to tell me something about Kelly, but I cut her off, explain the situation to her very slowly and clearly. She catches on fast, what with the threat of a murder charge hanging in the air. She is pathetically grateful to me, and to Kelly for footing the bill. I see the penny drop when she realises that help is conditional, and that's the last time she mentioned Kelly at all. In the whole course of events, Goodhall's name never came up once.

Sally pleaded self-defence on my advice, since there's no premeditation, no *mens rea* as we say, no guilty mind. In my business, you always stick to what we know you can get away with, assuming the moron you're defending doesn't fancy himself as star witness in Rumpole of the Bailey or whatever. (It's my biggest problem with the morons – courtroom dramas on TV that put stupid notions into empty heads. One bloke asked me once if I could get fucking Judge John Deed to defend him! I roll my eyes – 'That's Martin Shaw actually. He's an actor,' I explain patiently, 'and anyway he plays a judge, hence him being called *Judge* John Deed, got that?' The client thinks about this for a minute. 'Well, he must know a lot about the law then?' Need a lot of patience in my line of work. *A lot.*)

Anyway, to cut to the chase, Sally gets a hefty suspended sentence. The fact she was a tart didn't play well on the bench, but that's women judges for you. They hate tarts, insult to their womanhood or whatever. Who can fathom a woman's mind, eh? So, case closed and we all go home. Kelly pays up, Phillip does me proud in various ways, and things get back to normal. In fact, things get much better, because the Russians lose their grip on the disputed site and Givens somehow acquires the contract after a bit of monkey business I wasn't involved in. But the money rolls in big time and everyone's happy again.

Everybody except Bannermann. What with the trial, the extra business and whatever, we'd all forgotten about her. Then I start getting odd calls – she's been asking questions, even though the case is closed. I have a word with a few mates here and there, and it turns out she's going a bit of Sherlock on her own time. We make an official complaint – I warned Givens against this but Bannermann was taking far too much interest in the Elephant deal and she was making Givens rather nervous. Phillip too – he still wasn't in the frame at all, but I got the impression he thought the spotlight would eventually turn his way if Bannermann had anything to do with it.

So Bannermann receives a warning, told to lay off apparently. Does she stop? The fuck she does. I get calls from Freddy – a musician I know, drug dealer, represented him once for something unrelated – seems Bannermann has been hassling him. And a wop taxi driver who Freddy uses. Then Sally calls me, very nervous. 'Why does she keep coming round here, asking me stuff?' she wants to know, reasonably enough. I have no answer. 'The case is closed. Don't worry about it,' I tell her. Now *I'm* worrying about it. We all are, for one reason or another.

I can tell you exactly when things started to get out of hand. It was the week after a funeral, that woman Ivy I mentioned earlier. Everybody was there; Goodhall – she worked for him. Givens and his missus – guess they knew her though her husband Dan, who worked for Givens back in the day. Sally was there – what her connection was I have no idea. And Bannermann. Who the fuck invited her? Did she even know Ivy? I think it was just plain harassment.

Shaking hands with the vicar on the way out, I was considering the wisdom of making another complaint when Bannermann passes behind me. She stops, smiles at Roger Cornish – he's the vicar – and turns to Goodhall, standing on the steps waiting for me. 'Everything comes to those that wait, isn't that right Mr. Cornish?' The vicar smiles affably but seems lost for a reply. It doesn't matter, because Bannermann has already walked off.

I've said too much. You will hear other things, rumours and the like. To be frank, I just wanted you to hear my side of the story. I know there are some grey areas I've trespassed into from time to time, but Bannermann has me worried. I know these people. Like I told you, I come into contact with them all the time. I know when they are bluffing, when they go fishing. This was different. This was a woman with the smoking gun in her stocking top. She knew it. I knew it. So did Goodhall, to judge from the expression on his face outside the church that day.

I don't know what it is Bannermann's got, but I don't see how it can be connected to Sally in any case. Perhaps it doesn't matter. If they don't have anything, they'll fit you up. Then again, maybe it's another bit of spin she's going to concoct with her mates on the paper – journalists always suck up to the bill because that's who supplies them with most of their stories.

Either way, I have a feeling I'm going to be made to look bad, guilty by association. So I tell you this: keep an open mind. Things are not what they seem. Got that?

Famous Sword

I am called Viktor. Viktor Mieczysław (you say this mee-etch-swavna). I come from Poland.

My name has good meaning: Miecz is 'Sword' in my language, and Slaw is 'Famous'. So I – Viktor - am famous sword, right? How cool is this? Maybe you think I just talk big, but you ask Mr. Givens. He don't think so, I am sure of this, because he gets bad cut from famous sword, as I will tell.

As I am saying, I come from Poland. Tomorrow, I go back; I drive all the way in my new Mercedes. I know; you ask yourself obvious question, right – how does young Polack, only twenty-four, how does he get such expensive car? Sure I tell you, but you wait. First I tell story of my father, and why I come to England.

My father Max was famous sword also, you understand? He was pilot in Polish air force. Training as pilot anyway when Nazis invade. He comes to England at start of second world war with many others, so they could fight more after Poland was run over by Germans.

You know what? *They don't let him fight.* They think he is stupid because he is from Poland, is too young, and they think all Polish pilots are no good anyway because they don't speak English, maybe don't shave so much either. This? Stupid bollocks. My father, like many who escape, fights Germans during invasion. Even before he gets to England, he shoots down five Germans. Polish training for air force was best in Europe. Good pilots, bad planes – but still shoot down many Nazis. Anyway, RAF make Poles sit on arse, do nothing, no flying, training - nothing. So my father waits. He tells men, 'We wait now, you see – they need us soon'.

And he is right. After phoney war, things get bad. Very bad – not kosher at all. Germany is ready for invasion and sends huge planes to bomb England and fight RAF. This is Battle of Britain I am talking of – July 1940. Soon, RAF runs out of posh schoolboys, so at end August they get very desperate and call for cavalry. Poland is famous for cavalry, and my father leads many flying Poles into big battles. They come to rescue of RAF, just in time – like cavalry in John Wayne film, you understand? Cool!

He gets many medals, my father. Shoots down sixteen German planes, is ace. Is 303 Squadron my father is in, this named after big Polish hero General Kościuszko. You know, this squadron makes highest number of kills – 126 I think – of all fighter squadrons in Battle of Britain, even when they only join battle half way through. Poles better pilots than RAF, right? My father is big hero. Meets Churchill, shake hands. *This* is my father Max. (He tells us many times that never one single bullet hole was in his plane, ever, but I think he makes this up. This is OK though: I love my father very much and he is always big hero to me, bigger than John Wayne even. Anyway, he make stories better even if little bits not so kosher, so I don't care).

After war, he comes back to Poland thinking he is big hero. Big shock instead: communists arrest him as he gets off ship, torture him a bit, steal house and money, then send him to shit-hole work camp in Russia for twenty years. He is mad, angry and gets in trouble many times, fighting everybody – guards, police, other people in camp, and some monkey-business I think – but in same camp he also meets my mother, is fourteen year old girl at this time. She hates him, right off, which just make him try harder to get her. She just hates him more all the time, slaps face, kicks – I think she spits on him one time also. Hates him, always did, whole life. Just learned to love him at same time. Funny woman, my mother.

So now we are jumping forward. Is 1980. My father is in England, has own company, doing well. He has agency, gets men for jobs in building – brick and concrete work, building people – wood, electric, water – you know, this is trade people, know what I mean? Does well, company gets big. Has lots of contracts, and in 1984 gets job for company building factory in Russia. They send him to Leningrad to oversee work, because many Poles work for Russians and they need translator who understands this job.

One day, he goes for lunch in restaurant that makes good Polski food, and he is amazed, absolute amazed when waitress is my mother, woman he hasn't seen since camp. She never goes back to Poland, see. She recognises him straight away, throws bowl of soup in lap accidental, you understand? (This is what she says, right? *Accidental*.) My father say he grins like idiot with wet trouser, thinking love and hate not very far apart. He used to tell me, 'Viktor – love and hate like wheel of bicycle. You put finger on outside of wheel, turn and turn and you come back to same point. Love is half way round wheel, hate is on opposite side. Both on same wheel, always meet in middle. Hard to know where one start, other finish'. Spot on. (This is how my father thinks my mother loves him and hates him at same time, see.)

This time is different. My mother gives in, not like in camp. Maybe she stops pretending all she has is hate, that there is love too, just as strong. Two weeks, is all time they get together. Then my father has to go back to England. He wants my mother to come, and she makes big fuss saying no, no – but she tells me later she feels desperate to come too.

So my father does a fuck stupid thing. More monkey business. He comes back to London on own, very sad sure, but he is so crazy sad he does deal with Russian mafia to get my mother out of Poland. How does he know Ruskies? Because he did deal with them also to get him out from camp, send him to work in port on Black Sea so he can hide on ship, escape to England. He knows these people, has paid them many times over and now is free of them. So what does he do? He goes back for more Ruskie monkey business, and this time price is very high. 'Sure', they say, 'we get her out for you'. I only find all this out later, you understand.

Two months go by, then my father gets call – she is here! They get married quick. All is good for while, but then Ruskies turn up one day in office and take control of work, make my father use their people – stupid Latvians, Russian bad people, criminals, make him use these instead of people he wants, good people who know job. He complains, so they say 'be quiet or we tell people about wife'. They take money from him, from men, from everything. Steal everything from building sites, even tools from own men – not that men know how to use, know what I mean?

My father is honourable man, you understand? He is ashamed but he must honour agreement. Afraid also, I think. This is normal, even for hero. He keeps mouth shut, and four years this is going on without my mother knowing terrible price he pays to get her here, to keep her. If she was knowing, she would not make so much trouble: when I am five, she takes me back to Poland. Leaves my father, says nothing to him. Just goes one day, takes me by hand to train, then ship. My father follows us, but mother says no, we don't come back. He goes away very sad and angry.

Later, he comes to visit many times, bring nice things, tells us stories from war like I tell you, but always goes away again. I am sad many times. It is always same. He comes, we are happy. Mother is happy, and loves him. Then, after maybe two days, three – anyway, is always exact same. Arguments first, then throwing things. Smash dishes on kitchen floor. Screaming. He never touches her, though. My father – tough as steel and fight any man down to floor, but never hit woman, not ever. I know my father. This? Ridiculous bollocks mate, you understand me?

Poland was strange place when I was kid. Solidarity won elections year before I arrive with mother, and Poland is changing fast. We lived many places, my mother always looking for work in better place, more money. When I was small, Poland is grey everywhere, grey with communist concrete and big coats from Russian soldiers. But all changes. I remember shock to see tourists with cameras and Benson and Hedges cigarettes in gold box. I had empty gold box for years, very proud. Eaten by dog.

I also remember first time I see Mercedes. And BMW. (Porsche OK too, but Ferrari is silly like too big toy). All these cars like something from space, you understand? So shiny, so quiet too – Mercedes only, not BMW when rich people go past very fast to make you jealous. I decide then to get Mercedes, glide along so quiet with dark windows so no one can see who I am. *If I live that long*, because I am skinny boy and everywhere, big boys beat me up. All the time, I come home with blood on clothes, or wet all over where I try to wash off in river. My mother is very angry, like always, but she does wonderful thing. She takes me to man who teaches boxing and martial arts. Tiny man; old, so quiet. Could break pile of bricks with hand. Very kosher teacher. All the time I spar with him, I never hit him, not once. So quick, but like...like water, you know what I mean. Slide away so easy, very natural. Very cool – also like water. Hey mate, I make joke by accident! Thing is, he taught me well. Yes...he taught me very well...many things.

Now is five years ago. I am doing well, have good fights and win most. Also learn computing, love it straight away. Poland is very good, has many good schools that teach well. I go to school, learn programming and other good things, some things not so good also – monkey business, know what I mean? One day, two men are waiting outside school. 'Come with us, please' they say to me, but I don't think they really ask. They take me in car to Russian restaurant and I meet hard-faced man who tells me terrible thing. My father...Max...*my father is dead.* Murdered! In England.

I do not believe. They show me newspaper, with picture. It is him – most terrible moment in whole life. I don't think is possible they could make me feel worse, but I am wrong. My father owes these people very much money, they tell me. Impossible amount. 'Why do you tell me these things?' I ask them. I think I am crying. 'You must pay us back, now your father is dead' they tell me. '*Me*? I am fucking student, I have no money', I tell them. Now I am shouting, ready to fight them. But they don't want to fight me. They laugh and back away, laugh at me as I cry and shout all at same time.

When I calm down, they tell me I have choice, see. I must pay back money, or do something for them. Help them. 'How can I help you?' I ask, and now I am frightened because I know what these people do, what they are like. But they give me surprise. Big surprise.

'We want you to go to England. We get you job, at place we think is connection to murder of father. You help us find out who did murder and when you tell us, you come home. You do this and your father, his debt is paid'.

My mind is very strange sometime. One minute I am so confused, so angry and sad and afraid all at once. Nothing is clear at all. Then, suddenly: clear like pure water. Like ice has run in my head, everything is cool and sharp. I remember what old man teaches me, stillness at centre of storm like eye in hurricane, and in this stillness I understand: I will go to England, find out who killed my hero father. I don't know what I will do to this person, some murderer, but there will be time to think of this. Plenty time. You know, in that time while I am waiting, I have many terrible thoughts. I think about what I do to man who kills my father, things so terrible I am ashamed to tell. Maybe you know what kind of thoughts I mean?

But really this is stupid – you understand? I could not do any of those things. Not one. And now I know this for sure.

How does Viktor know? Because I do find out who kills my father.

After many weeks, the Ruskies put me on ship, so I work passage – cleaning, peel many potatoes, throw up and make more cleaning – but after many weeks I get to Hull and take train to London. I have papers from Ruskies, false but good, passport and work permit in new name: Viktor Polski (this is Ruskie joke, I think). I sit on train, look at flat land on east coast from window. I am surprised, because I do not expect England to look like this. So flat. (Later I go many other places and see country that looks like England I expect, like in tourist pictures).

People on train look tired. Not happy, which is surprise to me. This is rich west, right? Everyone is happy, has jobs, big house and Mercedes? – this is what I think from when I am young. But nobody speaks to Viktor and I am too scared to speak to them. Not even to get coffee. I try to be invisible.

It is beautiful day, sunshine and warm. Very nice. At station – Kings Cross – there are many people all in big hurry. I get McDonalds and I think, this is taste of freedom. (Later I think maybe taste not so good). I have instructions on bit of paper, it says I am to get tube train to London Bridge, go stand on bridge to meet Ruskies.

I find entrance to tube train, but there is a man with arms out who says is full up on platforms so nobody goes down stairs. I don't mind; I have time and think, this is chance to walk and see London, which I don't see in tunnel, right? So I buy little map, start walking south. I am excited. I remember sun and people, many buildings and so many cars, but most I remember sirens. Lots of sirens. 'Is this London always so full of sirens?' I am thinking to myself.

I walk for maybe five minutes, come to big square and see something strange. There is woman standing on corner of street. Nice dressed, like person who works in office, holding bag. She looks at nothing. Her face is dirty, grey all over, like she is dead person. Hands also, and clothes. Hair has grey in it. She looks like she forgets where office is, like she is lost. Behind her, down side street, are more people with grey faces, clothes. Some are sitting beside road. People walk like ghosts, you understand? Spirits, don't know where they go or why.

I see man crying, he is shaking so hard he cannot keep on feet and falls over, like boxer who doesn't know he is knocked out but legs give up anyway. Many people are at other end of street, cars stop everywhere. Smoke is coming from somewhere, thick black smoke. Bad fire, looks like. The woman I see first never moves, just stares at nothing at all. She really does look dead, except eyes still blink. I think, I will ask her if she is OK, maybe help her, but then I remember I am invisible so I turn away and keep walking through square. Now there are so many sirens I cannot hear anything else, and this makes me very nervous. Is this police looking for me, I think. This? More stupid. How they know I'm here? Why so many police look for Viktor? Crazy, man.

I am at edge of square now, walking slowly because I want to run and know this is bad. Behind me, there is noise I will never forget, like coke can when you stamp on it, but this can is size of building. Dull sound, but I know what this is – explosion in small space, inside space. Something small hits me in back, not hurts but quite hard.

I turn round to see what is hit me, but I see red bus in square maybe 200 metres from me. Smoke is coming from many broken windows downstairs, but top of bus is gone. *Just gone completely*, with big piece lying on ground in front of bus. One side of bus is sticking out, like top from open can of fish. People are screaming, some run past me away from bus, cuts on face, bleeding. Others run to bus, shouting mad. Everyone is very frightened, this is obvious. I stand still, do not know what to do. 'What hell kind of place is this'? I say to myself. 'I come all way from Poland for this? Is worse than anything I see back home, much worse'.

Now there are so many sirens, ears hurt. Police come in all directions and I think, 'Viktor, you stand here and they catch you, only have half a day in England then get sent home. Ruskies probably kill me for being stupid. I turn away and walk south, and keep walking. I do not look back. This place, I learn later, is Tavistock Square. Date is July 7th, and I remember this date all my life. Viktor, welcome to England.

Next day, Ruskies get me from house they own in Lewisham where they take me on first day. Complete shit-hole, 10 men to room. Filthy everywhere, stink of Latvians. Anyway, they take me to building site.

'This is where you work from now on,' they tell me. I laugh. 'I know nothing about buildings,' I tell the men. They laugh more than me. 'You in good company then,' they tell me, and push me out from car. One points to big man with beard. 'Talk to this man', he says, and they drive off.

Big man with beard is Gotthard, another fucking Latvian other men call Goat Herder (also sheep-shagger. I laugh very hard when I find out what this means). Actually, I would like to tell story now about what a shit he was, how he beats me with whip and is very bad man, but then I make things up a bit like my father for sake of good story. Truth? Goat Herder was OK, bit tough and drunk most of time, but he treat me OK, give me work that is not too difficult, so I don't look bad and lose job like stupid Latvians.

He is clever, this sheep-shagger – makes everything look OK when two men do all the work for ten other men, who just fuck about and do monkey business all day. I like this work too. I make building site into gym, do all jobs like training; lifting, running, pushing, pulling, work arms, legs, stomach, back. Get stronger, stay quiet out of trouble. Invisible. Think about finding man who killed father.

I tell Ruskies I will not stay in house. They don't care, I think. Maybe they know I do not run away, and of course this is true. I go to work every day, work hard, find little room near to job at Elephant and now I have home in England, I am settled and I start to think about my real job. But I am very lonely too. This is first time I feel this way, I think it is because of real work to find killer, this makes me secret, afraid to be friends in case I say something wrong. I just want to be invisible, but people do not make friends with invisible man, right?

I do not drink with other men from work either – most are stupid anyway – but I go to local pub sometimes for drink, best when I get old Polish newspaper from some man at work. This I like: quiet pub with beer and paper and sandwich. Feel sad but in nice way, know what I mean?

Thing is, one night in pub some men make fun of me, of very bad English I speak. They see newspaper and say bad things about Polish people. Ask if I am also four by two, and I do not understand this yet – I learn this cockerny speech later – so some man says to me 'are you Jew?'

I shake head. 'I am catholic' I tell men, thinking this is not their business. A man spits on floor, says terrible thing about Pope. Now I am angry but remember I must be invisible, so I leave pub and beer and paper (sandwich is finished). They follow me. Now I am getting very angry. For first time in England, I feel like stranger nobody wants. I am not bad person, so why do they treat me so bad, so rude all of time? I think of Ruskies and get angry. I think of dead father. Of home, and big debt I must pay before I ever go back there. Of mother. Most angry ever in my life, you understand? I turn to see four men from pub. I know they want to beat me. I am ready to fight them all. Whole country maybe.

Then it happens again, like I told you from before. My brain is ice cold. I think of old man, of silent peace in warrior. I take all this anger and hold in, like cold tight spring. The men surround me but I do not wait. I take the biggest man and hit him twice, perfect timing. He drops, holding head. I kick man behind in balls, then move between last two and deal with them.

But now I lose it, and I start to beat on man on ground. I think I am screaming. I look back now, know I was going to kill this man, maybe kill all men, but suddenly I feel arms come round me. Strong arms, but not other men from pub. A voice is saying things, quiet things. It is kind voice, not full of hate. The arms are not to hold me. This is different, like they are trying to protect me, protect me from myself. I cannot explain to you this thing, but I felt love in these arms. These arms belong to priest, Mr. Roger, and I think he saves Viktor's life that night, not from men, but from Viktor.

His voice is still in my ear, saying same thing over and over. Eventually I listen to the voice. It is saying 'you beat them, is OK. You won, you won. You beat them, OK...' I relax and he lets me go. The other men are helping each other. Mr. Roger says to them in hard voice: 'Go now. He beat you good and can beat you some more. Go away. NOW!' He shouts last word and they run like little boys.

We both laugh very hard. Then he takes me to boys club he runs, gives me tea and we talk. He is so kind, and no funny stuff – no God, no touching me – no monkey business. Just tea and sympathy. (This is what he always says: 'Tea and sympathy, is all I got'). After this I go to church all the time. I am catholic, he is England church, but he don't mind and I don't care.

I make new friend, and he get empty seat filled in church (there were lot of empty seats). Seems fair, know what I mean? I also make another friend at church, wonderful lady called Ivy who is dead now. I miss her very much, because she was also kind to me. I think this is because we were both such a long way from home.

I never went to funeral, you know. This makes me feel bad. Is not right, not kosher, for someone who is so nice to me. Not respect for dead. But nobody invites Viktor, you understand? I only get to find out a week after when Mr. Roger tells me she is dead. 'Why you not tell me this before,' I say to him, but he will not answer. This was very strange to me, but I know why and forgive him now. He does this to keep Viktor away from certain people, bad people, right?

Of course, it is in gym in boys club that we become friends. I think maybe my eyes go bright when I see training machines, full size ring. He grins, says if I want to fight, this is good place to do it. I laugh, say 'who I fight – these kids?' I am pointing to young kids in club doing exercises, playing pool. 'No no', says Mr. Roger. 'You fight me. I don't think you find me so easy like men from pub.' He has big smile, but I am thinking 'this is mad. I cannot fight with priest. Dear Jesus, *hit a priest*?' This? Fucking mental, mate. Serious.

But he is pulling me to ring, finding gloves, taking off jacket. He is wearing trainers like me. We put on gloves, get in ring. I am still thinking I get banned from church by Pope himself if I do this, but Mr. Roger is coming at me, and he is moving well.

'Wait a minute, Viktor' I say to myself. 'This man knows...' but I don't finish thought because Mr. Roger has hit me six times in two seconds and now he is helping me get up. 'Never let your guard down in the ring, and not very often elsewhere' he says to me, huge smile (I remember this exactly, learn it to heart).

I am not smiling at all. He is not priest to me now: priest don't give to people uppercut, hook combination. We start sparring but I am not angry for long. He is good boxer, clever, watches all the time. We have excellent session, great respect on either side (I do get own back for punches but he just smiles more, says things like 'nice work'). After, he says he learns to box at university, wins medals. I think this is true from what I see. He asks me after where I learn; he is impressed by my boxing – he tells me this – which makes me pleased. I tell him about old man, and Mr. Roger asks me to teach him old man style in return for free use of gym and machines, anytime.

How can I refuse this man? It is the start of strong friendship and many good sessions trying hard to beat each other up. This is not so strange: love and hate on a wheel, always spinning. Sometimes is just hard to know where exactly you are on this wheel, know what I mean?

So I am working on site, work hard, mouth shut but ears open wide. First surprise I find is that this site is not run by Ruskies at all. Only Goat works for Ruskies, is secret. Rest are from Mr. Givens. In fact, everything is from Mr. Givens; all men, all wood and concrete, metal, wire, toilet, sink, pipe – from everything he has hand in, Mr. Givens makes a lot of money. Like Tesco.

Then one day, after maybe two months, I hear men talking about my father. I am actually bit surprised to hear his name. It makes me jump because I only hear 'famous sword' first time, and think 'oh no, they find me out'. I turn around and there is man talking about my father, and how it is better when my father is boss instead of Givens.

'What happened to this man?' I ask them. I am shaking. 'They got rid of him,' says one man, and gives me strange look. I know what he is trying to tell me.

'He got in way,' says another, with same look.

'Who got rid of him?' I say to men. They will not answer; these men are good men, know jobs and do all real work. (Probably make least money on whole site, these are only honest men here. This is not good thought, right?) They look around, worried and suspicious and walk away from me fast. I cannot get them to say more on other days, but I have enough sense to be invisible and do not ask questions any more.

But this is the only time I can connect building job to my real job. I do not understand why the Ruskies want me here. There is nothing much going on except normal work for me and normal monkey business for everyone else. Now it is Christmas. I spend night in church but strange, I am not sad.

Then, after new year, Goat calls me into hut. 'You know computers?' he asks me. I nod – Ruskies have told him this. 'OK,' says Goat. 'Tomorrow you work here.' He gives me piece of paper with address down Walworth Road. 'Just how many days?' I ask him. 'Permanent,' says Goat.

Next morning I go to address. Is flat converted to office, nice but bit flash, cheap flash. Like stuff in market. Woman comes in, says 'come with me' and takes me to room with many computers, most in racks. She is dressed like flat, in stuff that says cheap sex; slit in tight skirt, big hair, many bands on wrist and gold chains round neck, big rings on many fingers, silly high heel, thick makeup, blow-job paint on mouth like too-ripe tomato, huge fake tits that never move at all, like some shelf to put dinner on. Perfume like fog. Not sexy, just she think too much about sex.

This is Kelly Givens. 'You know how to fix this?' she says, pointing to one PC. I fix it – simple problem with Windows. 'Now this one,' says woman, who is watching me like hawk. This one is not so simple – has little worm, not bad – but quick enough I kill it. 'Good,' says Kelly. 'They said you'd been well trained. This is your job from now on – you keep these machines going all the time.' Only much later I find out that last person to have this job had accident so bad he need to go find cure in America. Or else. Tough shit, mate. I don't care. It is how Ruskies get me where I wanted: the computers belong to Mr. Givens, Mr. Goodhall and Kelly. I work for them ever since.

First is just computer stuff. Then taking things to different places, just message boy really. But one time, Mr. Givens comes to boys club to see Mr. Roger, and sees me fighting with vicar. He is very surprised, asks why I say nothing to him, like we have big chats all time or something. Anyway, this leads to fight with Lenny, which was first time I made good money – two large as cockernies say – two thousand pounds.

I send to mother, she is screaming down phone with worry first, then happiness. I tell her: 'Viktor is success now, sends money'. She says: 'you do not get this money from fighting, right?' So I lie a little, is right thing to do I think.

Now I do little translation work for Kelly too, talk to Polish girls who work for her, and this turns out to be most important thing of all. Kelly is like many women who like fighters, get hot between legs at sight of blood and violence, likes sweat and men fighting. Kelly is like this, cannot keep hands off me. So I do little servicing as part of job, but she is fake as everything else in bed and I have trouble not to laugh at concrete tits. Feel cheap. Me *and* tits. But I am spy, right? I do my duty and fuck her few times, although I regret this very much now for reasons I cannot tell you.

I *can* tell you this. Givens is fuck dog lazy. One day he sends me to Mercedes showrooms to get papers for car he just bought. Brand new, 85 large – *with tinted windows*. 'Fill in registration and send off', he tells me with wave of hand, like king. So I do, in my name and using address of church. (I feel bad about Mr. Roger, but he does nothing wrong so no trouble for him I think). Papers arrive at church, Mr. Roger gives to me with funny look but no questions.

Tomorrow, I get in car with papers in my name and I drive home to Poland. All I must do is meet with woman tonight, police woman. But now it seems this is hardest of all things I have done, must do. To pay debt for father, to get killer, to settle score and go home, first I have to do something so terrible I am not sure this is possible. I have to betray my father, because it turns out famous sword cuts both ways.

Donkey Rides

Basta! Fuck you couriers! Insects! I squish you if you don watch out.

You see this? Terrible, these damn idiots. Such big bikes, such little dicks; this is what I think.

Sure mate, I know Bannermann. Nice legs. Look, I don say no bad things about peoples but that Freddy, he deserves what he gets. Pepi is honest man. I drive to right place, no monkey business going one way when place you want is other direction. Most of my fares are round here – go to pub, come home from pub. Go to supermarket, come home from supermarket. Is all boring, normal stuff. But Freddy, he calls one time and I get job. I go to pick him up and he gives me package, small – not heavy or nothing – and tells me where to take it. He gives me address on bit of paper, and gives me money for fare. This is good – not so good is taking package to place they don want to pay when you get there. Fuck, this is no good for sure, bad situation for me.

I take package no problem, go straight there, no pickup for other peoples first, which is what some do. No, I go there, deliver package – is to place near Harley Street, house of crook lawyer. I go there many times. Freddy likes me, he always asks for Pepi and he sends many packages all the time. Pays good, tip included – very important, mate – Freddy treats people right, is OK. Is steady work, so I am happy, but also I think: 'what is in packages?' This is normal, right? Anyone thinks this. Is not important to me, but I am thinking all the time like any person.

Anyway, some night I pick up fare from Manor Place nick. Is Bannermann, right? I am normal man, I look in mirror sometimes. Sometimes I see things you never believe, I tell you straight. Not this time.

'You keep eyes on the road' she says, not horrible or nothing. 'You Pepi?'

I say yes, sure I am. 'You deliver many things for Fred Smith?', she ask. I say no, because I don know this person. 'Fahrenheit Freddy', she says, and now I understand. 'Sure', I tell her. 'He is good customer'.

'You know what is in packages?' she says. Now she is leaning forward, arms on front seat. I smell nice perfume. I tell her truth, I don know what is inside. She laughs. 'I didn't think so,' she says to me. 'You are OK, so I tell you something. You must be careful with packages. Who knows what is in them. Next time you get delivery job for Freddy, why don you call me and show me package? That way no police car stops you, does search.'

Basta! Fuck you buses! You ain't so big, eh? Mind my paintwork.

Look mate, I understand things. This is not suggestion, this is orders. I think fast, drive slow. Sure, I agree with her and she gives me card with phone numbers. I reach destination and she gets out. I keep card but I never call her, honest.

You know, I don want no trouble, right? Who needs it, trouble? So you understand why I might worry about packages, why I might take a look inside one? This is what happens. Next time I get job for Freddy, I take package and stop in garage, get nice pie with some coffee and I check out package, open careful – is not difficult, I tell you.

Inside? I find drugs. Fuck, this is no good, for sure. I am bloody donkey...no, mule I think. Yes, Pepi is mule taking drugs round London in cab, just like idiot fucking donkey, no shit. They catch me with this, I get in big trouble. All the time I am driving nervous, looking in mirror, waiting to be stopped by police.

Nothing happens, I get to destination and deliver package. This is last time I take anything from Freddy. I am very angry and I think I call Bannermann, but this is no good. Maybe she arrests me too, or sends me back to Sicily. Or I have to go to court. I don want to get Freddy in trouble, not with police. I am angry with him, but not so angry I become grass. This is not right. In Sicily where I come from, we don talk to cops. We deal with problems on our own.

Funny thing. I pick up fare in west end, is Freddy, going home. This is OK, no packages, right? I say nothing to him, just talk about weather, usual English thing. We get to Pullens, and before I drive off Freddy comes back to car. He is so angry, white like a sheet. He jumps back in cab, points down road. 'Quick, quick' he tells me. 'I am robbed. Go quick, we catch them.'

I drive fast, across Walworth Road into Heygate estate. This is bad place, we don take no fares from them or Aylesbury – too many drivers get mugged. But we drive in – Freddy is shouting at me to keep going – and we see man with guitar running into flats. Freddy jumps out, chases man. I get out of car, lock doors and follow, don know why but I think maybe something bad is happening.

At bottom of stairs I find Freddy. He has caught man, is beating him bad. Kicking, punching, shouting, I think maybe he kills this man and gets Pepi in trouble too, so I pull him off. 'Come with me' I say to him. I am pulling his arm to car. 'Come home, Freddy. You have guitar now. I take you home, please?' I do not look at man on floor. He is bleeding, not moving. I think maybe he is dead, so when I hear moaning from this man, I thank God. We leave, and I take Freddy home.

After this I tell boss I don take no more jobs for Freddy, not ever. Give work to someone else, I tell him. He don ask no questions, just nods, so that is that. But now I am mad at Freddy two times. This man is serious problem for me, and I am angry because I do nothing but drive cab, and he makes big problems for me. So I find card, and meet with Bannermann. Why not? Drug dealing is bad thing, make junkies and this man lives off them, turns them into slaves. I think I have good reason to talk to Bannermann.

'Ah, Pepi,' she says to me. 'Now you don take packages any more, is no good for me. No evidence' Of course. Idiot! She needs package, right? I think of this, but say nothing. 'Too bad,' I tell her. 'I just try to help you, like I help him in Heygate last week.' She looks at me hard and I realise I say too much. Is accident, really – I am not thinking what I am saying. But now is too late.

'Heygate?' she says, too quick. 'Last week man was nearly killed, beaten up. You know who did it Pepi, don you? You tell me now.' I think I must look guilty when she says this. She is very hard woman; hard face, hard eyes. I feel scared, so I tell her what happens.

'You will say this in court?' she asks me. I refuse right away. 'No way,' I tell her. Pepi is not grass.' We argue but in the end she lets me go. This is last time I talk to police – always trouble, these people.

Later, I hear that she shows photo of Freddy to man who he beats up. Is good enough for arrest, and maybe Freddy goes to prison for little holiday. And I have plenty of work and no more hassle. This is fair, right?

OK, here we are. Police station. That's thirty-five pounds please...ah, no – I make same little joke last time, right? Sorry mate – six pound thirty.

Courage and Convictions

This sounds daft I know, but I didn't think Chinese people had a sense of humour. Yep – just sounds daft, don't it? But that's what I thought, I kid you not. I dunno how I could have been so ignorant really. Must be 'yoof' as the kids say these days. What on earth is happening to the Queen's English, eh? Is this how kids speak nowadays? I get text messages on my phone sometimes that are like code, no idea what they mean. I usually have to ring them up to find out what they were talking about. What's the point of that?

I never thought that about black people – that they had no sense of humour – but I reckon it was because in the films you always saw negroes with huge grins, mouths full of white tombstones...ah...sorry...it's the tombstones. Just comes to mind, all these connections with death.

My wife – she was Chinese – she passed on. Now I feel dead too. They say in time the numb feeling will pass. They don't know how much she meant to me, that's all I can tell you. Oh my gawd – why can you never find a clean bloody hankie when you need one? Ivy – that's my wife – she hated waste. She'll always be my wife, come to that – *she* wouldn't countenance throw-away things like kitchen towels or paper hankies. Until I got her out of the habit, she used to put so much starch on my handkerchiefs they wouldn't bend; ever tried to blow yer nose on a white bathroom tile? God, she was funny.

And that's what I was saying, wasn't it? Sorry, I keep doing it, just drifting off into little thoughts of her, little pieces like snapshots. It's like it was one big picture of our life together, and now it's broken into all these pieces and I can't put it back together.

The worst of it is that if I stop hurting, it will mean that I've stopped seeing the pictures in my head, and that seems like a betrayal to me. There's been quite enough of that in my life already. But I know her well. (Should I say that? I shouldn't, apparently; I'm supposed to say *I knew her well*). She would be sitting here, pouring tea into her little gold cups, telling me sensible things, like getting on with me life. I know that, but I don't want to get over her, because to me that's like saying I don't love her any more.

In the pub, talking about getting over the loss of a loved one, someone called it healing. I decked him, and felt bad about it afterwards, but for a moment 'healing' made it sound like Ivy was an illness, some infection or something, and I just lost my rag. I want to keep her picture sharp and clear, as much as it upsets me, but it's fading already. I feel like I'm deserting her. It isn't fair, none of it.

Dear me, what was I saying? Yes – never saw Chinese people laugh when I was a nipper. In films, you'd see evil Mexicans grinning under a 'tache the size of my hedge out front (and about as badly trimmed). Germans roaring in their jackboots, Frenchmen chuckling in their cheese. Negroes – like I mentioned – negroes singing away, so happy to be slaves, apparently – typical Hollywood, ain't it? But Chinese people were always 'wishy-washy' blanks, never really showed much of anything. 'Course they seem inscrutable if you don't let 'em laugh or cry, just a quick bit of bowing and scraping. What is it they call it – stereotypes? Never liked 'em, so I was a bit put out when I found I had a few of me own. That's the first thing I got from my missus. That, and love. Not sure which came first, really.

The point is, she was witty. Smart as a whip, had a brain on her, no question about it. Spoke better English than I do, if I was honest. That's one thing that really made me laugh, although she used to get quite angry with me when I did; angry in a way I never quite believed, mark you. It was when we were out someplace.

She'd start doing the pidgin English; Missee Ivee, I used to call her. She got pissed at me because it was her bit of fun and she didn't want me blowing it.

God, I had a hard time sometimes, especially when she caught a live one, taking the piss without the poor wretch knowing it. All for my benefit, I realised – she did it to entertain me, like so much of what she did. To please me, I mean. It was a competition really, to see who could please the other the most. I loved her so much, you know. Sorry; did I say that already? I keep repeating myself lately; don't know what's got into me, and that's the truth. Never been this soppy in my life, on my honour.

One time, I tried to explain 'ironic' to her. It started off with me chuckling away to myself over something I'd overheard, but I'll tell you about that in a mo. Ivy asked me what I was laughing about, and I tried to explain to her that something had happened that was bloody ironic.

'Like the metal?' she said, looking puzzled. Her little smooth face used to wrinkle up like a baby's when she was puzzled. Ah, it's making me laugh just thinking about it. We went on for hours like this and the thing is, I knew she'd really got it straight away. But no, she loved to wind me up, doing the Missee Ivee routine. The giveaway would always come when she started on the chop-suey dialog; at that point we'd burst into laughter, tears rolling down both our faces. Oh God, yes…tears like these…tears just like these.

Sorry, this is a poor show, ain't it? Let me tell you what it was that seemed so ironic. Thinking about it will piss me off big-time – it always does – and that will stop me weeping like a silly bloody girl or something, if you'll pardon my French. I'll stop swearing too. She hated that. 'Common' she would say, half under her breath but sharp enough I could hear. Ivy didn't like it, and I stopped doing it. So no backsliding, Danny boy; no backsliding now she's gone. The cat's gone, ain't coming back, so it's up to you now, Mr. Mouse.

I've never been the churchy type, but Ivy always was, ever since she was a kid, so she said. Her regular was the old place in Kennington Lane. I went with her a few times, mostly Christmas or Easter, and although I fell asleep a couple of times I didn't mind it much.

She chose this particular gaff because of the vicar – Roger's his name – who she adored. It was obvious, but it never bothered me because Roger was such a decent bloke, and he gave her something that I couldn't – that nobody could, I reckon. Whatever it was – some kind of spiritual thing I suppose – it made her very happy, and I was always up for that.

She loved Roger's sermons, which I thought were a bit weedy; I'm more a fire and brimstone man myself. Ivy used to say his sermon was like a soft pillow she could rest her head on when she felt tired, or a bit down in the dumps. She used to say the pillow sermons were very 'comfortable.' I think she meant 'comforting'. Maybe both.

Roger's one of the good guys. Straight as a die, he might be the most decent chap I've ever met. I knew him before I met Ivy, helped him with the club back when he first came here, got him a few choice bits of equipment, built the boxing ring with him, that sort of thing. I enjoyed his company, and it wasn't until much later I saw him box, which I have to say increased my respect for him a lot. Christ, he was bloody good...oops, that one just popped out. (Sorry, girl). Anyway, he was the business, was Roger. Still is – oh dear, now I'm talking about him like he's passed on too. The past and the present seem to get mixed up in my mind since she left.

Thing is, he told me about Ivy. Roger's not the kind of bloke who judges people, or says bad things about them. You have to fill in the gaps, so when he sounds a little disapproving, which for him is saying something, you can work out the bits he's missed.

We were installing a rowing machine, and talking about slaves in ancient warships, chained to the oars and all that. He said, right out of the blue like, he said 'slavery isn't over,' and then he told me about one of his 'flock' as he called it, how this woman was an orphan in Hong Kong, tricked into coming to England by a gang that terrorised her, got her to sign her life away, then stuffed her into a container in Hong Kong harbour with fifty others, half of them dying on the way.

Can you imagine how terrible that must have been? In all the years, Ivy never ever mentioned this to me, and I never asked – don't think I wanted to hear about it, and that's the truth.

When she finally arrived here, they made her into a slave, and for fifteen years she worked for various Chinese families without pay, long hours, beatings all the time. The low-key way Roger told me about it, the lowered voice all edgy – the story gave me the creeps, I can tell you.

'She's working for a Japanese family now,' he said. 'She comes to church sometimes with bruises on her arms and legs.' He shrugged, and I remember clearly how pained he looked, helpless. I wonder about his job – what can he really do? He seems to care so much, but there's nothing he can do most of the time. What's the point of that? He'll go to his grave an unhappy man, that one.

He told me all this stuff about Ivy well before I actually met her. That happened in the church one night, when Roger asked me to come over to help him fix a broken rail. There was no service that night, but Ivy had just popped in for a quick pray, and she was talking to Roger when I walked in.

I guessed who she was straight away. Roger introduced us, said he was making some tea and invited us to have a brew. Ivy and I exchanged a few awkward words, then we went into the little office Roger had and he gave us each a steaming mug of what I'd call proper British tea: dark, sharp, strong, drop of milk for the colour and sugared enough to hold off the bite.

We sat down, the three of us. Roger took a sip, as did I. It was lovely. We both looked at Ivy, who was staring down at the contents of her mug with a most odd expression – her face was all screwed up, just like I said: she was puzzled. 'What is this?' she says to Roger, who looks blank. 'It's...er...Chai...' he says, trying it on with the jargon. Ivy looked up at him, over to me, and burst out with the most beautiful, musical laughter. It went on forever, and that was it: I was a goner. I can hear it now and it breaks my heart, even as it lifts it.

Blimey! Uplifted? I've come over all religious. Get a grip, Dan. Actually, you'll like this. You know how true love is supposed to get the odd break, like in the films when some unlikely thing brings the lovers together despite all the odds? That happened to us, but to tell you about it I have to tell you about the other half of my life, about what I did before I met Ivy.

I'm known around here for my work as a corner-man – I train and look after a boxer during the fight. You've seen it on TV, course you have. Thing is, I didn't start out doing that. I started out doing rather nasty things, paid for by nasty people. Mostly, I worked for a man called Gary Givens. To put it simply, he's a gangster. He employed me to do exactly the worst kind of things you are thinking of, and I did them well.

From my boxing I understood the limits of the human body, where pain was felt most, which kind of pain – sharp, hard, continual, erratic; muscles and guts, nerve endings, fragile bones and other things – but this wasn't about fighting, nor was it about winning. My job was to keep people conscious so they could feel the punishment, suffer the maximum amount. I was good at it, which doesn't say much about me, does it? And what it does say isn't good.

Not just people either – they weren't the only victims. We smashed up flats, like over on the Pullens, to get people out. We trashed cars, shop windows. There were a few fires over the years, but I didn't have anything to do with that, not because I've got a problem with it, but because in my line, people don't die unless you get careless. In the firebomb line, anything can happen and I couldn't live with that – kids trapped, grannies on fire, that kind of thing. No way.

There. I've said it and that's that. I make no excuses. There aren't any. I was evil, and Ivy saved me. Half my life was as bad as a man's life can be, inhuman, as I see it now. I was indifferent to the people I beat up, the people I half frightened to death. Like a machine. That half of my life was bad, and that's the truth. This is the other half.

I told you this because you need to understand how Givens came to do me a big favour. I'd sorted out something for him, with a rather better result than he'd expected, and I knew it. We both did; in other words, he owed me. After, we were chatting away over a pint and I asked him if he had contact up west with the Chinese firms in Soho.

'Oh yes,' he bragged, like he always does. 'Know 'em all. Got some business going on right now, as a matter of fact. I saved their effin arses, the little twats. Got in a right mess with the City bill over in Limehouse and I got it sorted for them. They owe me, bigtime.' (He didn't say 'effin', obviously).

Thing is with Gary, he hates to be called out. I jumped on the opportunity and asked him if he could find out what it would take to release a Chinese bond-servant I knew. He was stuffed, couldn't say no because he owed me, and couldn't lose face neither, having done so much bragging just before. So I gave him the name on a bit of paper, and I have to admit I was very surprised when he told me a week later that he could get Ivy released. The price wasn't too bad and I had the money, so I gave it to Givens (and made him sign for it).

I didn't know how to tell Ivy – it seemed a bit rude, as daft as that sounds – so I told Roger. He was so happy I thought he was about to kiss me. 'Eye-eye,' I thought to myself, 'is he one of them, another bloody shirt-lifter in a dog collar?' But no, he just laughed his head off, then sobered up and considered what to do.

'Would you like me to tell her?' he asked.

Straight off, I thought that was a good idea. 'I'll give you the papers when Gary gets them off the Chinese lot,' I told him.

'No, you should be there,' he said. 'I'll tell her, but you give her the papers. You are her benefactor and she has a right to know you, and perhaps to ask why you did it. Have you thought about that, at all?'

See what I mean – smart, thoughtful bloke, ain't he? I hadn't thought about that at all. Maybe she'd think I was buying her contract, her next owner. That made my skin creep, I tell you straight.

The next night, I got a call from Roger because Ivy was in church. Apparently, she was rather upset because she thought she'd been fired from her job – the Japs had thrown her out. She had nowhere to stay, neither. Another thing I hadn't thought of. You can tell I'm not much in the way of planning, since things weren't going too well. The last thing I wanted to do was make her worry, poor thing.

I rushed over to the church and met Roger. There was something about his expression I couldn't quite fathom as he led me into the little office. Ivy was sitting there, holding her head in her tiny, careful hands. Her shoulders were shaking and she was making little whimpering sounds. I felt awful, really terrible and guilty too. I wondered if I'd done the right thing after all.

'She's very frightened,' said Roger. There was something false in the way he said it and I stared at him, but his eyes were on Ivy. She looked up, straight at me. Her eyes were bright and quite dry. 'Yes, poor little Chinee girl, she velly velly scared. You beat your new slave, meester? I be good for you, velly velly hard worker little Chinee girl, you see. Please you not beat poor little missee.'

The two of them broke into gales of laughter. Roger had already told her. This went on far too long for my liking, since it was making me blush – something I hadn't done for maybe thirty years. Ivy managed to contain herself and walked over to me, put her arms around my neck and gave me a smile so glorious I thought my ticker would pack up there and then.

'You are a wonderful man,' she told me, and kissed my cheek. I actually blushed again – a brutal bastard like me, blushing like a kid – and looked over at Roger. It was the happiest I've ever seen him, and I'm glad Ivy and I were able to share that moment with him. He deserved it, in a way I don't think I ever did.

It puzzles me – I've done such terrible things, yet she made me so happy; that doesn't seem fair when I think how unhappy Roger seems most of the time, yet how good a life he leads. It's not a fair world, is it? Perhaps that's why I lost her. Do you know, she never did ask me why I did it.

The trouble started when Givens gave Ivy and me a cruise in the West Indies as a wedding present. I couldn't afford a honeymoon, not after settling Ivy's bill, and we accepted gratefully. What we didn't know was that Givens and his wife Kelly were also booked on the same cruise, didn't find out until there was a knock on our cabin door, the two of them standing there. My heart sank, I can tell you.

We were five days out when I realised something was up – I'm not too quick in that respect. I'd been on shore, watching Kelly do a bit of shopping. She was really pissed off about something, and back on board, things were strange. Ivy was very quiet, withdrawn. I asked her, like you do. She denied there was anything wrong, like they do. A bit later, I realised there was something going on between Givens and his wife as well. We might have been on a polar voyage for all the ice floating around on the way back from Belize.

Only when we got home did Ivy come clean, and she was as bitter as I've ever seen her. It took a while to piece together what happened, but the gist of it is that Givens had threatened her. He had all the information, he told her, knew about her illegal status, her connection with the Chinese gangs, and threatened to expose her, have her deported, unless...the rest she would not describe, but I could imagine it all too well, since I knew what Givens was like. I thought of Kelly, the deathly chill when we said goodbye at the docks. A lot of things came right clear.

All of a sudden, Ivy was all over me, hugging me, trying to hold me down on the sofa – because I was about to go out and kill Givens. No question about it. Thinking about it, I suppose this is as good an example of what an amazing woman she was as I could ever come up with. Not only did she stop me – I'm...I was...eight stone heavier than her, for Christ's sake – not only did she keep me pinned there on the sofa, she calmed me down somehow, comforted me, and then she started whispering in my ear. Something changed in our relationship right there, I have to say. It was the first time I realised just how smart my new wife was, and how much smarter than me.

Time passed, we moved on and our marriage just got better and better. We didn't forget, but Ivy had a nice line in patience, and I learned a bit too. She told me one time that the mafia had got their 'revenge served cold' from Chinese traders who landed in Italy in Roman times.

'We said this two thousand years ago,' she told me, quite indignant that the Sicilians had nicked it. Another time she told me 'revenge is something that must brew, like my tea, to get the full flavour.' I said nothing, just kept drinking it, because that's what you do when you love someone that much.

A few months later, I got a call from Roger. Givens was going to manage a young boxer who trained at the church club, and he needed a corner-man cum trainer. I told Roger I'd call him back, discussed it with Ivy and took the job. From then on, every night when I got home it was like a military briefing, Ivy asking me all kinds of questions about the fight, the betting, training, rules, everything. I was stunned. I just used to sit there, gazing at her with big cow eyes like a dopey adolescent as I drank endless tiny cups of tea. I can't believe I actually miss her tea, but I do.

I worked very hard with Ali, the kid from Roger's club, making sure he got exactly the right results, because when you're bringing in an unknown, there's some big money to be made – or lost – on the early fights, when the form is still uncertain. We still didn't have a plan, Ivy and I, until I told her about how much money Givens had put down, how much he had riding on it, what with another firm wanting Ali's contract and prepared to pay Gary handsomely to get it.

Ivy saw it right off. 'You must go and talk to the men who want the contract.' So I did, discrete like, and cagey with it. I didn't really know what I was after, and I'm not sure Ivy did either, but the firm knew straight away.

'Givens has a great opportunity,' one of them said to me as we chatted away. 'His boy is worth a great deal to him, *unless he loses his next fight*'. There it was. Mention was made shortly thereafter about a side bet a bookie they knew might take, at surprisingly long odds. This was my payoff then – bet against Ali and make sure he loses, and I do well out of it. Of course, it wasn't the money I was after, but I wasn't about to turn it down. What's the point of that?

The mechanics were straightforward. I got some dodgy liquid stuff from this musician I know who deals drugs, and dropped a bit in Ali's water during the fight. He got clobbered, Givens lost his shirt, and the contract was cancelled.

Ivy and I celebrated that night, I can tell you. But Ivy also did something that made me love her even more. She insisted I give some of the money I won to Ali, and as soon as she said it I knew she was right. He was the innocent victim in all this – losing the fight like that. Not his fault, was it? He still had his career – which didn't amount to much – and he did sign with the firm that was after him, but just the same I bunged him a few thousand with a cheesy grin, telling him a good trainer always considers all the options, bets each way, some old rubbish like that. He didn't ask too many questions, smart boy that he was, which was just as well, 'cos I'm a terrible liar.

A few days later, I got a call. There was to be an investigation into allegations of doping. Givens had played it smart, getting a blood test straight away. Traces of the stuff I'd put in Ali's water were found, and when Ali made a statement saying I'd given him three grand, the interpretation was that I'd done it, which was fair enough if you think about it.

But Givens went further, producing two statements from ex-pros who I'd worked for. Both claimed I had offered them money to take a dive, to fix their fights. A complete pack of lies: this had all the hallmarks of Solomon Spang about it. The Board took a very dim view of me, and that was the end of my license. No more pro fights. It took Givens to get me back in the ring, and this is the ironic bit.

There's this woman – Andi, although she has another name sometimes – she's a good friend ours...was a good friend too, back then. One night while she was staying with us, we got a bit drunk – Ivy was out working – Andi asked me about losing my license.

I don't know why, but I lied to her. Seems daft looking back, but I told her I was framed, that it was this bloke we both knew called Pete Grippa who did it (he was helping me as a corner man during the fight) and that he'd admitted as much to a girl at the hostess club Ivy worked at, which was how I knew. It was a pack of lies, and I can't for the life of me imagine why I did it. And the thing is, she told Givens.

More time passes. There's a bad situation that Andi gets into, but it doesn't matter now. Ivy was very upset for a while, but things get back to normal like they usually do. Now, I like a pint at lunchtime; on this particular day I bumped into Givens in my local. He'd been waiting an hour, the landlord told me later, although Givens never mentioned it. He was friendly, cautious, said how sorry he was not to have seen me for so long. For Givens, it wasn't a bad act.

I asked him if he had something on his mind, and he produced an envelope which he slid across the table. It was a new license in my name. I'd been doing fights under an assumed name, but only small ones, or abroad, in case I was recognised. Now I could work again, the job I loved.

What price was attached, I wondered? This was 'Grafty' Givens, remember. It was to help him with this kid Viktor, who Givens was setting up for a big win and bigger winnings. 'I know it wasn't you, Dan' he said to me, very grave and serious. I nearly laughed in his face, and the urge to punch 'is head in wasn't far behind. He kept apologising, kept telling me how much he regretted what had happened, how he'd got it wrong. This was very strange, I tell you.

'Who do you think it was then, if it wasn't me?' I asked him, and when he said 'Pirate Pete' I had to bite my tongue. It wasn't until I got home and talked to Ivy that the situation got clear to me, because I have to admit I was pretty confused by the way things had turned out. It all seemed a bit unreal, somehow.

The outcome was that I took the licence – it was bent, but legal. That was my payoff. The deal was like Ali but in reverse: where Ali had been set up to win against big odds, this kid Viktor, who was really sharp, was being set up to fail against the odds, with all the punters convinced the fix was in the other way round. I went along, against my will I have to say.

This is one time Ivy and I disagreed – I won't say we argued, 'cos we never did. There was some lengthy to-ing and fro-ing though. She kept telling me the licence was what mattered, which didn't seem right to me. I did wonder if she sided with Sally – sorry, Andrea – or if she had something against Pete Grippa herself, but I decided I didn't care that much about any of it, and having the licence would be worth the few days needed to do my bit.

It all went to plan, the kid lost, I made enough from the deal to pay off my house, and poor old Pete Grippa was ruined, which was what Givens was after. Gary was pleased, made a fortune too, and I had my licence back. I thought that was the end of it.

I'm not a deep thinker. More a determined one, you could say. I just keep worrying away at a thing until I figure it out. Ivy puzzled me, and I had to make an effort not to screw my face up like she did because I couldn't stop thinking about it. In all our time together, I never distrusted her, not for one second. She was always so open, so straight with me – about everything. Yet I couldn't shake off the feeling there was something going on here, something she wasn't telling me.

Instead of asking her outright, I just kept worrying about it, because I was so afraid I might be wrong, I was terrified I could really screw up the whole thing just by asking the question. That would have been par for the course – get a wonderful woman like Ivy, who loves me for reasons I can't fathom even now, and then cock it up by being stupid. Story of my life. That's what stopped me asking, I think. I'd been stupid so blee...so often, it was like a habit. Like swearing.

I never did find out what was going on, but whatever it was, it was making Ivy enemies, and I knew 'em all. Freddy – the dealer I told you about – he was one. Givens and Kelly. Spang, the little creep solicitor. Pete Grippa was involved, as was Ivy's boss, Councillor Goodhall. She worked for him on the council before she died, after she packed up the hostess club.

How do I know? I keep asking myself the same question. It isn't like anything was ever said, but when she started getting ill I started noticing funny things. They visited her – all of them – coming round here with presents and stuff, like they were her friends. I didn't believe it – especially not Kelly, who had a hard job concealing what she was thinking, if you ask me.

We had visitors non-stop once the word got out she was ill. Loads of people, strangers to me, but they all knew Ivy. They brought food, offered money (that was embarrassing, I swear), flowers, chocs – I put on a ridiculous amount of weight because Ivy liked to watch me eat them, even when she couldn't manage one without throwing up – what else? God, loads of stuff; you name it, there was a packet, tin or box of it in the house somewhere.

So many people, and they all cared about Ivy. Especially one – Viktor, the young boxer I mentioned. Funny isn't it, the way things work out? He met Ivy before he met me, met her at the same church. Ivy really liked him, and when I came home one night and told her I was working with this young Polish kid called Viktor, she was amazed. Made me bring him round the next night for a meal, and we got on famously, although neither of us – me and Vik – mentioned the monkey business we were planning, obviously.

That's another thing about my wife. She was a wiz with the old computers – that's how she got the job in the council works department. Amazing, and that's the truth. Her little hands used to fly over the keys, and when it turned out that Viktor was another wiz kid there was no stopping them. Might as well have been talking in Chinese, those two. Gobbledegook ain't in it, but what I remember most is how happy she looked, asking all these questions. Young Vik knew his onions, real hot stuff apparently.

Towards the end, he was round here a lot. Surprised a few people, I think. The slags, I mean: I'm sorry if that sounds bad, but that's how I think of that lot now. Perhaps I shouldn't, because I was one of them too. I didn't like having them in my home, but what can you do? Thing is, compared to all the other visitors, all the nice people, there was something I didn't like about these visits. It was like they were all watching Ivy, coming round here to see how ill she really was. I tell you this – no word of a lie – I think they were waiting for her to die, the whole fucking lot of them, and no apologies this time for the language.

They say her heart gave out in the end, but I don't believe it. She was so ill, getting worse no matter what the doctors did for her. They pretended they knew what they were doing, having her in and out of hospital, all the tests and stuff. They didn't have a clue if you ask me. Bloody doctors – yes, *bloody doctors* is right enough too. They couldn't admit they hadn't got a clue, too proud to say it.

Mind you, they did everything they could think of, and I think it made her worse. After several weeks in hospital I took her home, discharged her myself even though they kept telling me she should stay in that grim ward with its smell of piss and death and filthy floors. I just wanted to make her comfortable, and home was the best place for that.

I didn't work, didn't go out – didn't need to really, so much stuff turning up at the door all the time from well-wishers. Roger was a real brick, came round every couple of days with little gifts of his own, always thoughtful and kind to me, chatting with Ivy for hours when I ran out of words and got too emotional, which I knew upset her even more. But the others, the slags – no idea what they were up to, but I tell you this: I think they had something to do with it. You'll think I'm mad, but I can't get this thought out of my head, and I told Bannermann the same – she's a DCI down at the nick – I told her I thought there was something funny going on, but I didn't know how to prove it.

Something killed my wife, and it wasn't natural, I don't care what the doctors say. There's a smell of something rotten here, and five people I know seemed to have an interest in her dying that wasn't right, although I can't imagine what it could be since Ivy was the nicest person you could imagine. In the end, I don't care what the story was. I just know that these people are scum, and that they didn't care about Ivy at all.

I don't know what they were up to. I do know they deserve what they've got coming. Just like I do.

Long Legs of the Law

Mistakes we make in hours but regret for a lifetime.

That's my story, plain and simple. When I was just a leggy girl in SOCA – that's the Serious Organised Crime Agency – it must have been obvious I was good with numbers. I worked at an accountants for a while before I joined the force, and I remembered much of what I picked up. I was the one ending up ploughing through the books and paperwork of crims we nicked, gangs we raided, dealers and so on. I knew my way around spreadsheets and could manage data – it's important not to change anything that may be evidence, like computer accounts, and I didn't bugger anything up, which helped.

I didn't have problems with the men. Frankly, joining the force and expecting an easy ride is stupid. I don't understand the women who complain about the men, I really don't. It is a male-dominated force, and I knew that before I ever joined up. I was expected to do better than the men, to prove myself to them. It isn't very fair, but what is? I got on with it, and earned respect, earned my place on the team.

It is probably true that because I did a lot of the dull grunt work figure-wise, (although I don't find it dull at all,) they were grateful, but only to a certain extent. On a tough team, they don't carry passengers. And look – I'm not being cynical when I tell you that men are a bit weak. Show 'em a bit of leg, look a bit soppy while you're asking a favour; most of them will cave in now and again. God, I love 'em; wouldn't have them any other way.

On the morning of my birthday – that's how I remember it – I heard about a chance to work on a case team at the Serious Fraud Office. They employ all kinds of people and they aren't part of the force, but they do use us in some situations, especially where there's an overlap between organised crime and their work. My guvnor was a really nice bloke and offered me a shot at it. Strictly speaking I was too young and inexperienced, but he put in a good word and they seconded me, on probation as it were.

My first task was to familiarise myself with the casework. There was a ton of stuff in various forms – computer records, accounts, databases, pictures, paperwork – so I scanned everything, labelled it as best I could, and put everything into a database we use, including all the text and all the information on invoices, dockets, delivery notes, that kind of thing. The reason I did this was because the database is designed to look for connections, the same thing appearing twice in seeming unconnected files. After a few days of this, I got a hit: a name. And to my lasting regret, I knew this name all too well.

A year or more before I went to the SFO, I worked on a case connecting a property racket to a local gang, ran by a thug called Gary Givens. In connection with my investigation I was required to interview a local man who owned several of the properties we were interested in. His name was Phillip Goodhall, a local councillor, influential in Labour circles, and something of a party animal, from what I heard.

I conducted two interviews with him. He seemed respectable enough and we had no reason to believe he was involved, so nothing more came of it. Now I sat, staring at the screen and Goodhall's name, with a flashing asterisk beside it – flashing because the program had found a connection.

I read the files more carefully, took notes, documented my procedures, and it seemed to me there was a clear link between the company who had transferred money to an account held by Goodhall in respect to a property transaction, and the international money laundering operation the case notes dealt with.

Now I admit I didn't discuss this with anyone else, which was a mistake in hindsight, but I was new: I didn't want to make a fool of myself so it seemed important I check my facts first. Later, people called it a private witch-hunt because of the secrecy, but it wasn't. It was just the caution of a woman trying to climb a man's ladder without getting too many runs in her tights.

I started doing extra hours to sift through all the material. Nobody questioned this; they just thought I was bloody keen, which I was of course. I talked to mates on the force and revisited the SOCA case notes many times. Out on the street, I had contacts I'd cultivated, and a few arms were twisted here and there, metaphorically speaking. A picture emerged, and it became quite clear to me that I had been taken in by Goodhall.

Worse still, I realised how he'd tricked me, but I'll come to that shortly.

One of my 'regulars' was a Pole we called Max the Sword. He was run by the local Russian gang, and we both knew that some of the information he gave me was passed on behalf of the gang; disinformation for the most part, but with a few tips on the opposition that were worth acting on. The trick was to tell which was which. Max was the one who told me about the Elephant redevelopment and the connection with the council works department, which Phillip...that is, Goodhall, ran.

This was the real thing: finally, I had something on him to take back to the Office, something meaty enough for them to investigate, because the SFO don't bother to get out of bed for anything involving less than a million quid. That's what makes them *serious.*

I never got the chance. The next morning I was called straight in to the Chief Investigator's office. The head of HR was there as well, as was a solicitor called Solly Spang. I was not invited to sit, which was a bad sign. It got worse – they knew about my investigation and before I had time to explain, they accused me of conducting a vendetta.

I cannot tell you how shocked I was, really. This slimy little creep Spang – who worked for Goodhall and Givens, it turns out – had accused me of perverting the course of justice, of all things. In front of my guvnor, he had the nerve to accuse me of persecuting Goodhall for personal reasons. 'What are you talking about?' I demanded. 'What personal reasons?'

Spang gave a vile little smirk and turned to my boss. 'Mrs. Bannermann had a very brief affair with my client, Mr. Goodhall. A one night stand, you could say. However, Mr. Goodhall is a married man, and thought better of his position after straying from the marital bed for a single night. He felt ashamed that he had responded to this young woman's advances, advances made in a wholly unprofessional way during a needless second interview, an interview conducted entirely under false pretences I might add.

My client then informed her that he would not see her again. I regret to say that Mrs. Bannermann did not take this well. My client subsequently received numerous phone calls, letters and emails...' He reached into his posh briefcase and pulled out some papers, handed them to the Chief, who studied them.

'Did you write these?' he asked me, handing them over.

I looked very briefly at them, and denied it flat out. 'They are forgeries,' I told him straight off. I resisted the urge to ask him how stupid I would need to be to write anything down like this.

'Did you know Mr. Goodhall? Did you have any contact with him?' said the Chief.

It was Goodhall's word against mine. 'I met him twice, during the course of an investigation. That was all.' My voice was flat, professional. I can hear the words echoing round the room.

I looked at Spang, who smiled like a snake and reached into his briefcase again. 'In that case, can you explain how my client came by this photograph, which he gave me earlier today?'

He passed a picture to me. I looked at it, handed it to the Chief Inspector and walked out of his office to clear my desk.

I have never been a foolish woman. I'm down to earth, I work hard and very little impresses me. But Phillip Goodhall, well – he was something else. The first time I interviewed him, I remember I was in a bit of a strop over something or other. I started giving him a bit of a hard time, and I have to tell you he was so charming he actually had me laughing by the time I left, my mood completely changed.

There are some men, some few of them, that just melt you from the inside out like a microwave. Phillip was one. He was attentive, thoughtful, witty; had a nice line in self-depreciation and above all he knew how to make a woman feel feminine without insulting or patronising them. He was good looking, smart, well-dressed and well spoken, and he had this habit of tilting his head to one side when he was puzzled in a boyish way that didn't seem contrived, just rather endearing.

He didn't underplay his intelligence though, and when pressed he got smarter rather than crack under pressure, coming back with good retorts and answers that seemed both logical and truthful. In other words, he was a professional politician in the making; credible sincerity, and the moral flexibility of the rank opportunist.

The second interview? Well, I do wonder about that. I'm sure looking back on it that I did have a good reason to interview him again, but I can't say for sure there wasn't some personal motive, some interest in seeing him again. You can't help how you feel. I've known good solid coppers drop their pants in circumstances that make you wonder if they forgot to put in their brains when they left for work that morning. It isn't corruption, it's human nature, and if we lose that human nature we become the worse for it. There are lines you cannot cross, but calling it 'sleeping with the enemy' is going too far. Goodhall wasn't the enemy, not then. He was just someone we talked to in the course of our enquiries.

I'm not making an excuse here, but my marriage was a bit rocky at the time. I was under pressure at work and at home, all at the same time. My kids – I have a son and a daughter – were both getting in trouble at school, and my husband was away a lot, being the chief surveyor for a big firm. It was hard to cope with, and the force isn't that sympathetic to women with kids, so you have to do a juggling act and hope you don't drop something. I never was much of a juggler, I suppose. Things are fine now, kids doing well and my husband and I are happy, more or less. Normal, in other words.

The day I visited Phillip the second time, I have to admit I was out of sorts over my home life. I did something unusual, in that I called him first and arranged to speak to him that evening, instead of during the day. No big deal, but since I was off duty at the time, when he offered me a drink I took it.

I hadn't dressed up especially, although I had put on a dab of slap here and there just to cheer myself up. I asked a few follow-up questions, but he kept changing the subject, talking about how hard it was for a woman to have a decent career. He seemed to understand very well how tough it was to get on, how much harder you had to work just because you have tits. He made some comment about sexual harassment, I remember. I told him I hadn't really experienced it, apart from the odd bit of bum-pinching, which the boys did deliberately as a wind-up, not a feel-up.

'They must be mad,' he said. 'I'd be after you all the time.' It was so cheesy and so obvious – not really like him, as if he'd dropped the normal act, quite candid in a way, disarming and a bit clumsy – and the way he said it was rather flattering. I had another drink and...well, I really don't need to spell it out, do I?

He was a good jump, I'll give him that. Full of cunning little tricks. Christ, I was exhausted – out of practice, what with the situation at home. I remember clearly lying there in his bed all damp and sweaty, propped up against the mirrored backboard having a drink. Phillip was sitting on the end of the bed, fiddling with his phone. I remember it because I got quite demanding, made him drop the phone and repeat his performance, which he certainly did. Jesus, I was sore the next day. It wasn't one sided either; he was limping when I left, I promise you. He'll have more than a fucking limp when I'm finished with him.

So that's what the picture showed. He took it with the phone: me, slumped up against the wall, my boobs hanging out for all to see, and in the mirrored bed-head you can clearly see Goodhall perched on the end of the bed, stark bollock naked.

The rest of it is rubbish, made up by his pet toad, Spang. It was me who realised what a disgrace I'd made of myself. Goodhall called me a few times, and I told him in pretty robust terms what to do with himself. His wife had come back from the states by now, and it took the threat of telling his wife to get the idiot off my back. After that, I just put it out of my mind, I promise you. I didn't spend all this time building a career, only to throw it away over some dickhead with an agile tongue, now did I?

Getting transferred to Manor Place took a little sorting out, but if I was going anywhere, I wanted to be on the same beat as Goodhall. And Givens – I hadn't forgotten about him either. Talk about the long arm – now they were about to find out what it was like to have the long legs of the law around their necks. I'll bet you anything you like it ain't sexy.

Sometimes we underestimate people. I hadn't spoken to anyone at SOCA for a while because I expected to be something of a pariah. They called me in the end, and we all went out and got very pissed. They could smell a rat when one crawled up the drainpipe, and they were bloody supportive, I can tell you. During one riotous scene in a karaoke bar, one of them told me something very interesting about the Elephant development and Givens, a turf war between him and the Russians.

'There's a connection you might be interested in,' my mate told me, shouting in my ear. 'It's Goodhall's office that put out the contract they are fighting over.'

The next day, despite a headache the like of which I never want to repeat, I couldn't get this out of my mind. I started doing a little sleuthing on the side, much more discretely than last time. And this time, it really *was* personal, I promise you.

There was this woman who worked for Goodhall. Her name was Ivy, and I knew her because back in the SOCA days we were looking into gang activity, and her husband Dan was *known to us*, as we say. He was a hard man, violent and brutal, and he was Given's enforcer – the man they sent round when you didn't make your payments, or whatever it was you were supposed to do. Thing is, after Dan married Ivy I went round to their house several times in connection with incidents that had all his trademark violence about them. Twice, he denied all knowledge and his wife, although she didn't say much, did give him an alibi. Means nothing, of course, but there's little point in trying to pin anything on a villain like him unless you have something substantial. I had sweet FA.

The third time I went round, Dan was out. Ivy invited me in none the less – she was very polite, I remember – made me tea and sat across from me in the lounge. I didn't know what to say to her, how much she knew about her husband's line of work. Anyway, sometimes the best interrogation method is to say nothing and just wait. Sure enough, and without prompting, Ivy broke the silence.

'Dan is changed,' she said quietly as she passed me a dainty little cup. That was it, all she said. No protestations, no explanations, nothing. It was impressive, so sincere I really had to believe her. On the force, you develop a sense for these things, I think because when you meet so many outright liars, you learn the patterns of their pathetic lies. Perhaps that's why I fell for Goodhall; he had no patterns.

Ivy was right, as it turned out. Time went on, we came to realise that Dan had retired. Nothing we could do about the cold cases; since he didn't show up on our radar any more we left him alone.

Thinking about Goodhall's contracts reminded me of Ivy again, so I went to see her one day. I waited until Dan went to the pub at lunchtime – I knew he was a regular – and Ivy and I sat and drank some lovely tea from her dainty little porcelain cups with the gold rims. I told her about my investigation, and said that anything she told me about her work would be treated with great confidence.

I was wasting my time. She never said a word, just listened politely and poured tea. No, she did say one thing – and it puzzled me quite a bit. I was telling her about some of the property scams, the money to be made demolishing old buildings, when she looked up from her tea.

'Ah, the Pullens,' she said. 'You are investigating Mr. Goodhall.' She opened up then, the only time she ever did, telling me about the goings-on at the Pullens, most of which I already knew – the fire-bombings and the harassment, the beatings and forcible evictions. She never said how she knew all this, nor did she say outright that Goodhall was involved, but the message was clear, and final. I wanted to ask her who her source was, but I didn't bother since it was obvious she wouldn't tell me in a million years. I rather liked her for that, actually.

Shortly after my visit to Ivy's, my boy Max was murdered, or got himself killed, if you believe the result in court. Max was alright, a good ol' boy, and it was a shame, although the situation did suggest he got what he deserved. The thing that made me suspicious about the case was that Solly Spang was involved. In fact, he called it in, and was on the scene when the investigating officers arrived. I wasn't there – not my beat, I'm supposed to be on robberies and car ringing – but I heard he stuck very close to the girl who stabbed Max. I didn't get to talk to her until after the trial; I did keep my nose to the ground and heard some interesting things, but nothing much came of it.

The next thing that happened was one of those odd connections. It's because the crims are a local community, so there's always strange ties and allegiances, debts and enmities. This is the bread and butter of my work.

Here's an example: there's this taxi driver, Italian chap called Pepi, and he'd been ferrying drugs around London for the local dealer. He claimed he didn't know what was in them, although he's dropping these strange packages off all the time, picking them up from some punter in a flat. How unlikely is this? Doesn't matter, actually. I decided to have a word in his ear, warn him off.

While we were having our little chat, he said something very interesting: Ivy and Freddy the dealer, who lives on the Pullens estate, worked together in a hostess bar. It made me laugh, I'm sorry to say. Unprofessional, but the thought of Freddy being a hostess, with him in drag charming a bunch of drunk Japanese execs, was irresistible. (He was actually in the band, if you're wondering).

I decided to leave Pepi alone for now. There was something else on his mind, but these things are sometimes best left to brew. He'd only just found out that we were watching him, and knew what he was up to. That was enough for one night.

What I did do was visit Freddy. I already knew that he and I had a common enemy, because as Ivy had told me, Goodhall and Givens were trying to get him and his friends evicted. We hadn't been able to connect the evictions and the threats to the tenants back to either of them, but we were still digging. I also knew that Freddy's friends – travellers, anarchists, Marxists, indigents, hippies; you name a fringe group, they were involved – this lot had formed a rather effective residents association and were taking on the council. More's the point, they were gathering all kinds of information we didn't have, because they connected with the opposition in a way I could never do – by selling them drugs and doing a little fencing on the side.

So I did a deal with Freddy and his crew, gave them a lot of useful intelligence that was helpful in their fight to retain their tenancies and save the estate from being demolished, in return for everything they had – which turned out to be a damn sight more than we'd got, for Christ's sake. No question, these people were good networkers. I've had a sneaking admiration for them ever since – it sounds bloody daft, but they would make good coppers, some of them, if they could lay off the dope long enough to remember to come to work.

There was a bonus too. I don't know how he got hold of it, but Freddy delivered something unexpected when he gave me the dossier they had put together. It was an invoice, and for the first time I had a financial link between Givens and Goodhall.

My first reaction was pure delight, but this was rather squashed when the story about the now-defunct SFO investigation – well, my investigation actually – somehow got into the local papers. Of course, they all came after me straight away, Spang leading the charge, but I swear to you on my honour that I never gave them the story. I have no idea at all how it came out, but it sank Goodhall well and truly in his bid to become an MP. Christ, my blood runs cold even thinking about someone like him in parliament.

I say I have no idea, but I'm pretty sure the Pullens crew shopped Goodhall to the press. Can't say I feel bad about it, but I couldn't explain my deal with Freddy and had to take some stick for the leak. Not for the last time, I suspect, I was warned off and chastised for my failure to follow procedures, but the bollocking lacked conviction. Since everyone was very interested in the material Freddy gave me, the heat went out of the situation pretty fast.

The newspaper story did give us one advantage; it was a cage-rattler of considerable proportions. I wasn't the only one to realise this. I was invited on the quiet to the SOCA offices, my old stamping ground, for a 'chat'. Since I was out of their orbit, they 'suggested' that it would be good to keep the pressure up on Givens and Goodhall, turn up the heat. This was a bit cunning; because it was unofficial, if anything went wrong I'd take the blame on my own. No blowback for the SOCA team or the Manor Place squad.

I didn't mind, since I could think about little else now. I went to see the brass who killed Max, put a little pressure on. As for Givens, Spang and Goodhall, a mate of mine has a nice trick we used. He's a clever bod, an engineer who works for a mobile operator. He can do something technical to specific phones that makes them click at random times during a call. This really freaks out the crims, because they think their phones are tapped – like our actual taps would be so crappy. Still, we do like them to think they are; always good to be underestimated.

Then we put a few spare foot soldiers on watch from time to time outside Goodhall's house, Spang's office and Givens' place, making sure they got noticed. We tailed Givens' Merc a few times, just for a laugh. I have to say, they all looked quite rattled.

Then Ivy died.

It was quite a turnout. Hard to believe she knew all the people who showed up, but Goodhall's unholy crew were there. I rattled their cages a little more, then left because I wasn't going to be that disrespectful to Ivy. The vicar had already given me an odd look, although I didn't interpret it correctly, as it turns out, because a few days later he called me, asking if I could pop round and see him. He wouldn't say what it was about, but he's a nice enough chap, so I wasn't put off and duly paid him a visit.

How can I sum this up? At this point, we didn't really have the smoking gun. Lots of circumstantials, no killer punch. We might get one or the other, but not all of them. We knew Spang was up to his sweaty armpits in all of it, but we had nothing at all on him, not a damn thing. So basically, we were bluffing, hoping they would crack, the best odds being on one of them turning on the others to cop a plea. God knows, they were slimy enough.

They say good things come to those who wait, and they come in threes. The first was clearing up a nasty GBH assault over on the Heygate estate. I paid another visit to Pepi the taxi-driver, leaned on him a bit and he told me that Freddy had beaten up some kid. We showed the victim a picture, and got a positive ID in a line-up, so that was it. Freddy confessed and he's on bail now, waiting on the charge sheet. (Actually, if it were up to me, I would have left off and used the threat as a lever to get to his suppliers, but the decision was made to arrest him for the sake of the bloody performance stats, and that was that. Waste of good intelligence if you ask me).

But that was nothing compared to what happened next. As I said, I went to see Roger the vicar. We chatted for a bit, small talk, but I could sense he was winding himself up to do something, so I waited.

Eventually, he sighed and reached into a drawer, pulled out an envelope and placed it between us on the desk. I reached forward but he put his hand over mine to stop me. He had big hands; soft, gentle but quite firm.

'I must tell you something,' he said in that quiet, unassuming voice of his. 'I give you this because I have been asked to do so. I have given my word that I will not divulge who gave it to me. I want to make this clear to you, Marty. I know what's in there. I know what it means. I want absolutely nothing to do with it, and what you do with it now is entirely your concern. Take it away and study the contents. Do not look at them here, because you will be unable to resist the urge to ask me questions. Since I will not answer them, we can both avoid wasting what I expect will be an unpleasant hour if you just leave now.'

I won't keep you in suspense. This was the second good thing, and it was everything I could ever have hoped for. It wasn't so much a smoking gun: it was a bleedin' multiple-warhead nuke.

The third thing is a little depressing. At 3.45pm I arrested Dan Tucker on suspicion of murder. He walked into the nick, asked to see me, and confessed on the spot right there in the hall. The desk sergeant was as stunned as I was, but I had no choice. I took him to an interview room, got him a cuppa and started the video.

Now look, I'm not saying that people can't change, but it's bloody unlikely. Thing is, with our Dan, we all reckoned he really had changed and for the better. He'd been good as gold since his wedding, and everyone around this area could see for themselves how much he doted on her. They were always together, always doing things. He even went to church with her, apparently. When she died, it really broke him up. I mean, he was a complete mess at the funeral, couldn't stop crying. It was quite sad to see, even for a hard old tart like me.

Then the rumours started, all coming from him. Since they concerned the same group of people I was interested in – Givens, Goodhall, Spang, Freddy, and Goodhall's pet whore of a wife Kelly – she runs an escort agency, and a nastier piece of work you'd be hard put to find – these low-lives were on my radar anyway, so I went to visit Dan at home. Between sobs – Jeez, it was depressing to watch him – basically he claimed his wife had been poisoned by one or all of them. He couldn't tell me how, just kept repeating that it was all a plot, how they hated Ivy, but he had no idea why.

Now, I have to tell you that my personal radar just wasn't picking this up. For one thing, the doctors had treated her for weeks and they never found any signs, not that they were looking of course. But they signed the death certificate as natural causes, so we had no official interest in the case. Ivy was cremated, so we couldn't do any forensics now even if we wanted to. And as my guvnor said to me, the experienced hands know that sometimes, a bereaved spouse will be unable to face the truth, and start to invent conspiracies and crimes to make themselves feel angry instead of hurting so much. A kind of defence mechanism, I suppose. I have to say, that's exactly what I thought myself at first.

Here's the thing, though. When Dan showed up at the nick, I thought we were in for more of the same. Instead, he sits across the interview table, calm as you like, and tells me he did it. He got some 'stuff' as he called it and had been dosing Ivy for weeks.

'What stuff is this, Dan?' I asked.

'No idea,' he replied. 'I got it off some Russian bloke in a pub in Lewisham.' This of course is sounding more unlikely by the minute, except that Dan is dry-eyed, serious and direct, in a way that most people telling a tale can't manage. I remembered what my guvnor had told me, and wondered if this was a new version of the same thing: someone so distraught that they are prepared to take the blame for a death. Sounds odd, but so did Dan's story up until then.

What got me confused was when we started talking about motive. I asked him the obvious question, and he didn't hesitate. He told me about the cruise – we all knew anyway, bit of local gossip for a while spread by Kelly most likely – and he said something rather chilling.

'I wanted to kill Ivy there and then, when she first told me. Why didn't she come to me, tell me what Givens was up to? I'll tell you why. Because she liked it, liked being a whore. She didn't like being a wife, I tell you that.'

'What do you mean?' I asked, caught up in his story now. The camera was whirring away.

'We had separate rooms at home, that's all I'm saying,' he said, rather gruff. I couldn't find a context for this remark, so I left it alone and moved on. 'You decided to take revenge on her later, is that it?'

Dan nodded. 'That's right, I did. I waited and waited until I was sure she was up to something. I got suspicious, you see. Something to do with Givens, seeing how things went. Maybe she was going back for more, the way she was so fucking keen for me to work for Givens again, especially considering what he was supposed to have done.'

I took a break right there, wanting very much to consult somebody else. I saw Dan banged up downstairs and found my boss. Over tea, I told him what Dan had said, and showed him the video. He sat for a while, tapping his pen on the desk top in a bloody irritating way. Then he said a few things that I have to admit did make sense.

'First off, you've got some local villain, a right thug, who falls for some exotic woman he doesn't know, hasn't even met, and all from a distance – never even spoken to her. Doesn't know her from Adam, but spends a fortune buying her contract from the Chinese gang who brought her in. Why does he do this? It isn't like they are having it off, some burning affair, is it? Think about it – Dan's the sort of bloke who might well think that if he has the papers, he can call the shots. He's purchased himself a bride, right? Never mind what she thinks, either. To her, he's just the next owner.

'So he coughs up the dough, and pressures the poor woman into marrying him. Maybe she thinks this is a better bet than being beaten by some Jap family. Who knows? Anyway, they get married, and go off on their little cruise. She has a fling with Givens, apparently while refusing to sleep with her new husband. Now he's the mug who not only paid out for her contract, but is being humiliated by his wife having it off with his boss – and on their honeymoon, for Christ's sake – at the same time she's making him sleep on the couch or whatever.

'How stupid might a man feel in those circumstances? How un-thanked and unloved? With a villain like Dan Tucker, that's enough to get you killed. Frankly, I'm amazed Givens is still walking around, if the story is true.

'And with a thug like Dan, if the rage doesn't come out straight away, where does it go? It festers and glows in the dark, leading to something terrible, some eruption of anger and passion later on or, as in this case, revenge. Maybe that's what happened here, by the sound of it.'

In the end, I had no choice. I cautioned Dan, filled out the charge sheet and they shipped him off to Brixton prison. I passed the whole thing on to the Crown Prosecution Service. They can sort it out now, decide if there's a case to answer. I have to tell you, I'm still not sure. This is one time my radar doesn't seem to be working, so I'm going to get a couple of G&Ts down the local, then go and arrest a few people who I owe a visit, a kick in the crotch and quite a few years behind bars. I'm going to enjoy this a lot.

Men Play the Game, Women Know the Score

Well, I guess we should get right to it. I don't have much time left. My name is Phillip Edward Goodhall. I am forty-four years old and I run the Southwark Planning and Building Control department, with considerable influence over the way the four billion pounds of regeneration money is allocated. I'm also an utterly corrupt politician, councillor, and have made a great deal of money through rampant fraud, as have many of my acquaintances.

Have I shocked you? How quaint. If you find that shocking, wait until I've told you the rest. I know candour is hardly common among people like me, not when deniability is everything. But not today, not now. My time is nearly up, leaving me just enough to tell you my story.

And do not think I look for sympathy, or seek to excuse my behaviour. There will be no expiation of my guilt, for I am no penitent. I have no regret and no remorse. I just did what we all do, the difference being that unlike most of my peers, I got caught, that's all. The invoice for my culpability has come due, and there is no way I can defer payment.

I have always loved women, and they have often loved me. I say love, but that's a slippery concept, isn't it? Sometimes it's passion or lust, sometimes it is pity or need. Companionship is a factor, so is loneliness. All these things, these motives and requirements, they get tangled up so much it's hard to determine which is which, or how one really feels. I love the intimate warmth of a woman's body, the smell of sexy sweat, the candlelight romance and the knee-trembling quickies. I love their waywardness, their caprice and greed, their innocence and their guilt, their blatant manipulation and their copious – and often indiscriminate – generosity. Wonderful creatures: they have destroyed me utterly.

They say that love is blind. I always fancied I was the one-eyed king, but that appears to me now like just another deceit, self-deception on a monumental scale. What heights I have scaled, only to look down in terror when I realised there was no way to climb safely back down again. In part, this is why I am being so candid now. There's a great scene in a film – can't remember the name offhand – but it's Peter O'Toole and Kate Hepburn being gloriously over the top. She's Eleanor of Aquitaine, he's Henry the something (I forget the number, but it isn't fifth, that much I can tell you). James Goldman wrote it, although I can't remember who the director was either.

This isn't like me, you know; I have excellent attention to detail, usually. It was a Broadway play originally, like so many good films...aha! I've got it – The Lion in Winter, that's it! Great film, and because it was taken faithfully from the play, an excellent adaptation – which makes it all the more frustrating I can't give the director the credit he's due – the text shines because it reflects the importance of the words over the image, as one must do in the theatre, when you can't jump cut from scene to scene, place to place like you do in films. I prefer films that have a literate text; Shakespeare in Love, Equus, Robert Bolt's work like Man For All Seasons, or even The Philadelphia Story, although that just looks like a filmed stage performance. Kate Hepburn again – wasn't she gorgeous? My kind of...no, that's silly. They are all my kind. That's my problem.

As I was saying, there is a scene in which Henry's sons have been locked in a dungeon and expect to be executed. One is Prince John – later the scourge of Robin Hood if you like – and Richard is also there (this is before he becomes the Lion-heart). Damn it!

Now I can't remember the third one either. Too bad; minor details now.

Anyway, there they are in the dungeon, arguing as they do all through the film, and they are talking about noble deaths – their own, of course. Richard is all warrior indifference, staring death in the eyes and all that. Prince John is cynical, mocking.

"As if it matters how a man falls down," he taunts his brother sarcastically. Richard stares at him with great contempt and replies: "When the fall's all that's left, it matters very much".

This is my fall.

The assassination of my idealism came, funnily enough, around the same time I started taking drugs. The connection may not be what you think. Like so much of what we think, we are conditioned into thinking drugs are just an escape, like getting pissed. I don't know what it is about our culture; the transcendental use of intoxicating substances is ancient and venerable, but we are so wrapped up in our fear and self-righteous judgements we cannot countenance such things. Do we fear the genetic past, some atavistic notion of ourselves that is far more animal that civilised, tamed man? I suspect it is still an echo down the ages, the conflict between free people – hunter gatherers – and settled people, but that's a pseud's diversion.

Drugs then; they can transport you. The trouble is, most people don't realise that there's no free lunch. Really; because you buy the stuff doesn't mean you are going to get the real benefits just by taking it. Doesn't work like that. I use marijuana and cocaine exclusively. When I take them, it's like being presented with two doors, only one of which you can pass through. One door is marked 'indulgence' and leads to sitting around, quite off your head, probably talking crap or lying around in a semi-coma listening to music, stuffing chocolate down your throat and going 'wow, man!' at regular intervals.

The other door – and hardly anyone chooses this – the other door takes you to a harsh place, where the object is to surf the waves of your consciousness, your awareness, see where it goes, pick one wave and see how far you can ride it before you fall off. The hard bit is to catch the damn wave in the first place. Quite often, you are left standing on the beach with nothing but a can of beer in your hand and a vague feeling there's something out there, but that you missed the boat entirely. The one that got away.

If you *can* catch the wave, lock on to it, then the drug is the surfboard you ride on. It's usually a thrilling ride, emotional, scary sometimes, and all the while you try to keep your balance, which is hard if you travel at speed. So the challenge is to see how far you can go, how far before you fall back to Earth.

And yes, I know the old argument. Sure, you can do this without drugs, given the time and effort and dedication to a discipline that will get you there – you hope. But let's be realistic here, shall we? Life is short. I can't be a monk, chanting all day in between imitating fighting animals. I have to work for a living, we all do. We just don't have time to explore everything we might wish, so expediency is a necessary evil if you want to gain speed, travel further, learn more. Isn't that what life is supposed to be about?

Speaking of being realistic, the wave I rode was generated by reading The Prince. It wasn't the drugs that destroyed my youthful hopes. It was reading The Prince. Do you know it – Machiavelli's work? It is the definitive guide to expediency in the service of power, and I found it revelatory, compelling and thoroughly practical. It should be the handbook for every serving politician, but none would admit to owning it, let alone reading it, because the realism of the study is so utterly cynical. It reminds me of another line in that film: Henry says "I've plotted all my life. There's no other way to be alive, king, and fifty all at once".

That about sums it up, I think. Before this little epiphany, I had believed that things could be changed. My teenage folly – save the whales, ban nukes and stop wars – all that was expunged at Oxford. It was replaced by political activism, social militancy. We were serious young men having seriously lofty thoughts, and we believed we understood everything, could fix everything. Humorous, isn't it? Sweet, callow youth; such innocent and unlikely certainties.

After graduation, I went to work in the City. I started to build a network, get to know local people who mattered. I joined the Southwark Labour party, went to meetings, started making impromptu speeches and soon I was making a name for myself. A bit of a firebrand, a bit intellectual – which working class people love, you know, in a fawning kind of way – quite radical but charming with it.

That's how I think I came across, although I don't mean to sound calculating. That came later. No, this was genuine, just how I was at the time: fresh-faced, enthusiastic, idealistic. And very popular with the ladies, may I add. To be crude, if women's votes could be gathered by fucking them, I could have been a huge, if rather exhausted, success.

But as successful as I was politically, financially I was suffering. Campaigning takes money; entertaining is very important if one is to create the right impression. Success breeds success. As I learned early on, you have to appear successful rather in advance of being so. That way, people have confidence in you. Gaining that confidence is a constant drain on resources, and because things were going well, I decided to accept an offer of assistance.

An offer of assistance? Ah, how very ambiguous of me. Old habits and all that. What I mean is that I was so desperate to succeed, intoxicated by the success so far, so flattered by all the attention I was getting, that I committed a crime to get more money. That's a rather more straightforward way of putting it, isn't it? I did some washing at the bank for a man called Gary Givens, who I had known from my schooldays. And when I say 'washing', I mean laundering of course. Money laundering, the proceeds of crime made untraceable. Some of those proceeds bought me property and rentals and, most importantly, disposable income.

You step over the line thinking you can somehow step back again, put the thing back in its box. Now *that's* what I call idealism. Actually, no. And to be truthful, I never thought that. I'd read The Prince. I had no intention of closing the box again. This is how things really worked and I knew that now. Everywhere; throughout the world and throughout history. Deals get done, the wheels turn. Look at defence procurement; billions in outright bribes to despots and dictators. Same thing, bigger budget. If our government can do it, what the hell?

Anyway, it's how you get things done, and that is the point. I wanted to make my mark, improve our lot and enhance social justice, and I was prepared to use whatever tools were required to do so. The money was never for me, for my lifestyle – not much of it, anyway. It was to further my agenda, or to put it in an alarmingly simple way: to do good. My certainty has never left me, but my commitment to acting on it has faded in inverse proportion to the size of my bank account.

Ambiguity and inertia; these are the guiding principles of government. If we are not inert, then what we do must be ambiguous. The reason for this is understandable: we are terrified of public opinion because it is so well informed and so utterly pervasive. I don't know the real figures, but I'd hazard that media penetration has increased by an order of magnitude since the second world war. So many channels, so many cameras. The internet is everywhere, every second of the day, consuming news and propaganda and spewing it out instantly into a billion homes all around the world. A reputation can be destroyed in a millisecond – the time it takes to press the 'send' key.

You learn ambiguity – it's another name for deniability, isn't it? – to protect yourself, then. The carefully worded statement that sounds like 'yes' but only if you want to hear it, for nowhere does the word actually appear. If in doubt, deny absolutely everything, and do it with great conviction for the camera sees the lies very clearly. Learn the sound bites prepared for you, and repeat ad nauseum no matter what question you are asked. You have to be a good liar, a skilled one, a sincere one.

That's the game, and those who don't play it are destroyed by it. Perhaps the problem is that one conflates ambiguous sound bites with ambiguous morals. Perhaps it's also a bit late for me to think about it, considering the circumstances.

It is a blurry thing, politics, like shifting sands. That's also a good description of my relationship to women; shifting sands – lovely to walk on, but rubbish when it gets in your pants. Thinking back to what I said, the contradictions women embody are themselves ambiguous. There isn't a man alive who hasn't been completely baffled by a woman who may, or may not want you; need you; hate you; love you; save or betray you. To make matters worse, their disposition changes by the minute, on the minute. *Or not*, just to keep you on your toes.

Take Martine Bannermann, for instance. She was a bright young thing, a detective with a good financial head on her – I won't make the obvious joke – and she got curious about the property I owned. She was investigating Givens in fact, but my name popped up somewhere and she came to my house to interview me.

She was a fine little filly, headstrong and compulsive, and quite unloved. You could see it immediately, the way she was suppressing her femininity, I suppose because the more manly she appeared, the better her chances at work. The ironic thing is that all the others hated her because she was so butch and aggressive.

They used to call her 'Dyke-man', which for the police is quite witty, wouldn't you say? They gave her the drudge work to keep her out of the way, and when a chance came up for a plum at the Serious Fraud Office, all the senior men – and the women too, I understand – they all stood aside so she could be given the transfer, just to get rid of her.

But on this particular day, she was fragile and lost. She did the interview in a cursory way, but I could tell she was distracted. I didn't mean to come on to her, not really. I was just trying to cheer her up because at heart, she seemed quite nice, actually. Certainly nice looking. And she did perk up quite a bit, laughing gaily by the time she left. 'I may need to interview you again,' she informed me. There was something playful in the way she put it, as was the way she put a hand on my arm as she said it.

'I'm not going anywhere,' I told her, and I don't suppose I was all that ambiguous about it, either.

Inevitably then, when she called a few days later and told me she needed to interview me for a second time that evening, I made sure I was alone when she came. She was dressed to kill, quite lovely actually and very sexy in her heels – great legs, as I could see this time for she was wearing a skirt somewhat shorter than a detective should wear, I think – anyway, things progressed naturally and we ended up having a lovely evening. I even took a snap of us on my phone camera, although I forgot to show it to her.

The next day I saw Solomon Spang, my solicitor, showed him the picture and told him about last night's little escapade, just by way of an amusing aside, really. He was very alert all of a sudden, and he put several rather odd thoughts into my head. Was she one of those mad coppers who will do anything to find some evidence, even go as far as sleeping with the enemy? I didn't think so, because she had demonstrated very little interest in the case, and a lot of interest in my trousers, but I hadn't considered the possibility either and that bothered me a little.

I said I didn't think it likely – that was my genuine assessment – but Spang wasn't convinced. 'You should keep this photo of her. Just to be on the safe side, huh? And don't see her again; it's just too bloody risky and if Gary finds out he'll go nuts.' I could see his point – nobody in their right mind wanted to get on the wrong side of Givens. And keeping the picture was insurance; if anything came up, it might prove damn useful – as indeed it did.

What happened first was one of those things you can't predict. She called that afternoon, and I made some excuse or other. The next day, she called again but seeing the number, I didn't pick it up. She didn't leave a message. Then the emails started, funny at first and touching, but gradually becoming more insistent, more demanding. I had the sense not to reply, but I had to get this cleared up, and called her at work knowing what she could say would be limited by those around her. I just told her my wife was back and we should move on, nothing unpleasant, nothing dramatic. She said no, she wasn't jealous of my wife and was happy to be my mistress. I told her more bluntly that I didn't want a mistress, and that I really couldn't see her again. There was a long silence.

When Bannermann broke that silence, she really surprised me. She declared in a shrill voice that she had no intention of seeing me again, insisting the affair was over; this having begged to see me only minutes before. Now she was denouncing me in the most strident terms, angry I think because she realised she had crossed some line that she too could not step back over, and she was blaming me for tempting her to cross it. Typical woman, in other words. In seconds, she had switched from supplicant to judge, and I was found guilty. Of everything.

As the saying goes, 'give a woman an inch, and she becomes a ruler'. (Er...don't take the 'inch' too literally). Then the threats started, and things got very ugly, so I put down the phone and called Solly Spang. He was pretty sanguine about it, I must say. 'I'll make a few calls,' he said, and hung up.

I didn't hear from Marty Bannermann again. Things went quiet for a while, but then I started hearing *about* her instead. She had been transferred to the SFO. We learned that she had copies of absolutely everything she'd been working on and taken them with her, telling the others she was going to plug it all into the SFO system and 'pin me to the wall', as she put it. Like a trophy, I guess. This was around the time I was about to be nominated as parliamentary candidate for Bermondsey. The last thing I needed was a whiff of scandal, generated by a woman scorned: hell's fury indeed.

Now she was asking questions, and Spang reckoned it was time to act. He asked me to make two prints of the picture, which he took to the SFO offices one morning along with an official sounding complaint, in writing. Bannermann was dumped, the case was closed, and we all breathed a sigh of relief. Prematurely, as it turned out, because she immediately popped up again, transferred to our local police station.

Later, things actually got worse. She told the local papers about the thwarted SFO investigation and they printed it. The nationals loved it, and suddenly I was a pariah in local political circles. The nominating committee dumped me – can't say I blame them, frankly, since I was largely unelectable by now – and my career in politics was wrecked. I did manage to get re-elected as councillor, and of course I kept my job. It was my job that now got the full focus of my attention, since my true ambitions were stalled.

Just to bring this particular story to a close, I will tell you that Bannermann has kept at it ever since. And you know what? She got us. I am not so entirely lacking in grace that I will not admit I quite admire that, in a perverse sort of way.

I became a lot more ambiguous towards women after that, I can tell you. My strategy was to employ the same style of political ambiguity to my relationship with women as I did my campaigning. However, one day this rather worked against me, I'm afraid. I didn't make clear my lack of interest in a certain woman's charms – if indeed you could call them that – and she mistook my ambiguity for tact, seeing as she was Gary Givens' wife, Kelly.

I won't say Kelly was unattractive, but in a crude, blow-up sex doll kind of way. Not the kind of woman you discuss French cinema with, if you follow me. No, it was like being in a porn film, being with her; very little dialog and most of that the clichés of the rut, which she spouted endlessly with all the emotion of a cockney Satnav.

I regretted it even as we did it, and all the more when my wife walked in on us. My marriage wasn't bad; Andrea was a political asset, a good hostess, ran a good household even though she worked as well, enthusiastic in bed rather than skilled, but that was OK – plenty of skills to be found elsewhere. But Andi couldn't have children, and I don't think she ever got over finding that out. Our marriage was probably finished well before I was seduced by the rough charms of Kelly Givens and her awesome chest. How she didn't topple over is beyond me: I imagine her at the dinner table with her plate a foot away, just so she can see what's on it.

She was also the only woman I ever slept with who faked an orgasm, something I never quite forgave her for, although I will admit I was peeved I couldn't make her come – it was like she deliberately held herself back. Why would a woman do that? Do you see what I mean about them now? What fucking chance do we have, I ask you? Me – no chance at all. I'm sure it was my irritation made me go back try again after Andrea left me to become a fucking prostitute.

Now we seem to have reached the point where I confess all about my shady business dealings. This can be dispatched quickly; in my job, now I'd reached the top of that particular ladder, I could greatly influence where the contracts were going, for how much, and on what terms. The details you can gather for yourself if you like, but the point is this: to profit from such power, you need accomplices, and mine were my dodgy solicitor and Gary Givens, whose wife was screwing his business partner - me.

A volatile situation considering Givens' temperament, but Kelly was the kind of woman you cannot so no to after you have said yes, because she is quite unpredictable and has a badly-hidden vicious streak a mile wide and as long as the M4. Her most likely action once spurned would be to tell her husband. I did not underestimate her, as it transpired: she was a vengeful harridan of the worst kind. Much worse than I ever realised, as I have found out to my greatest cost.

Our most profitable venture was the development at the Elephant and Castle. £4 billion in government regeneration funds. A bucket so deep and so wide it was hard to know where to dip one's grubby little hands. Some days, it seemed like money was swilling around the floor of my office, so much of it was spilling off the edge of my desk.

Heady times, and more low-hanging fruit than I had ever seen in my life. Contracts were awarded with terms that allowed the maximum amount of loose change – this is how Spang referred to the proceeds – to fall into our pockets. We had overseas accounts and dummy companies all over the shop. I couldn't keep track of it all, and wouldn't have any of the paperwork in my house in any case, but I knew I was already worth over a million, aside from declared assets and interests I was obliged to register. And this was just the start, or would have been if Bannermann hadn't been about to close us down.

There was one fly in the ointment. Somehow, the most lucrative demolition contract went astray, ending up with a company we knew was a front for Russian criminals. Quite how the contract went there remains a mystery since I had made certain it was going to one of Givens' contractors, yet their name somehow ended up on the paperwork instead of the company I wanted. I have reason to believe that my secretary was in the pay of the Russian gang, and she made the arrangements, but that's neither here nor there, really. The point was that Givens and Spang blamed me. I said I would fix it, but actually there was little I could do without drawing unwelcome attention to myself. We were stymied.

Imagine my surprise then when Kelly raised the subject as she got off me one afternoon, her hair dank like a wet dog after a good run. It wasn't clear to me how she knew – I assumed Gary told her, but didn't think too much about it.

'You got Gary right wound up,' she told me as she crammed her monumental tits into a bra you could carry your children in. 'It's that bloke Max, ain't it?'

It was indeed. Max was a Pole running the front operation for the Russians. He controlled the site and was drowning in gravy, as Gary charmingly put it. Considering the lack of illumination in her vacuous little head, Kelly did manage to ask some penetrating questions about the contract and on what basis we could revoke it. Then she made a suggestion that took me by surprise.

'Suppose something happened to him,' she suggested, rather coy all of a sudden. 'If he was mixed up in something bad, something illegal. Would you be able to take the contract back?' I thought it was possible at least, and said so. With suitable grounds we had several termination clauses we could probably use, and Spang was a dab hand in that department, weasel that he is. You could almost hear the gears whirring behind Kelly's eyes, the calculation occupying her completely. 'I have an idea...' she started, but I saw this coming and stopped her. Remember, deniability is everything. What she didn't tell me, I didn't have to lie about later. Ignorance is akin to innocence in these matters.

'OK,' said Kelly, seeming to understand at once, which was unusual in itself. 'Leave it to me, love.' That was all she said about it, and I did just that. It's hard to say if this was the worst mistake I ever made, but it certainly comes close.

It would be pointless and quite disingenuous of me to pretend I didn't know how my business partners managed their affairs. Knowing as many people as I do, one hears all the gossip percolating through the local social arteries like so much tainted blood. From time to time, Givens was mentioned in the press – allusions more than accusations – but I washed my hands of the detail with a disdain worthy of Pontius Pilate. None of my business, and they had the sense to keep me out of it, since I was the golden goose and had to be protected.

But these were violent people and I will not pretend I wasn't aware of this. It's another part of the system, and I accepted that it was a necessary evil, just one I was not personally party to. At least, I wasn't until one night a few weeks later, when the phone rang at 1am, waking me. It was Kelly, and she sounded very strange. She wanted me to come to a house in a residential back street, an invitation I declined.

'You must come,' she warned me in a voice tighter than her skirt. 'If you don't, I'll have to call Gary instead.' I understood straight away; this was a clear threat and the way it was made left me in no doubt it would be better to see what the problem was than convince myself it would all blow over if I ignored it. Damage limitation then, which is always best done pre-emptively.

Have you ever seen a dead body? I hadn't until that night. I was shocked, but strangely excited too. I cannot explain this, and I feel a certain guilt when I revisit the sensation, but I will tell you that there was some frisson, an awful shudder of delicious power, overlaid with the darkest sexual overtones; that's what I felt looking at this dead man lying on the floor. The man was Max, and to demonstrate just how callous I have become, the first thing I thought – the very first thing – was that now we could get the contract back, had the grounds to cancel. To my eternal shame, the second thing I thought was of having sex with Kelly right there and then.

The third thought, however, drove any carnal thoughts right out of my head. I looked closely at the blood-smeared face of the unconscious woman, still lying under the dead body of Max, stabbed to death by the prostitute while defending herself from his beating. The prostitute was my ex-wife, Andrea, which as you can imagine was truly unexpected and frankly, quite unnerving. I felt my gorge rising and ran to the kitchen, vomited in the sink, then cleaned it up. (Kelly, cold as ice, wiped my fingerprints off various surfaces, trailing behind me until I'd recovered, while reminding me not to touch anything else).

As I said, I already knew Andrea had become a whore, to my great consternation. She had remained discrete though, and didn't appear to want to rock the boat. I was thankful for that, although the monthly direct debits probably helped. (If this wasn't blackmail, it was bloody close, I tell you). My wife, the blackmailer. The prostitute. And finally, the murderer. Fucking hell, it seemed this boat was sinking fast.

My entire career flashed through my head, as if I were dying. I felt quite a strong sensation of vertigo. 'What can we do?' I muttered. I was quite pathetic if truth be told. Kelly was like steel, and she scared me. This was a version of her I had never seen before, and it was as ruthless as it was cold.

'Call Solly,' she told me. I have to admit it made sense, so I rang him on my mobile and he came over straight away, parking near where I told him I'd left my car. I went to meet him and took him back to the house, showed him the bodies and let him ask a few questions. He thought about it a while, then made Kelly and I go home.

I don't know how he did it, and don't want to know, but by the end of the trial, the connection between Andrea and myself still had not been made public. Then Bannermann told the papers about the SFO investigation, and my boat sank anyway. I think now it was always going to sink with me as its captain, because every course I steered was crooked.

We carried on looting the coffers, but I kept thinking about what had happened. What on earth had Kelly been up to? What was her plan? I couldn't see the sense of it. We wanted to get Max out of the way, but killing him seemed so extreme I discounted it as a plan, and filed it as an accident – after all, there was no need to go to such lengths if a simple murder was the solution.

So what did Kelly think they could achieve by setting Max up with my wife? I should mention by the way that I was sure by now that Givens knew what was going on. I can't explain this, but I kept getting odd little looks from him, and instinct told me the rest. It is irrelevant really, except if you consider whether he and Kelly were working together. But if so, what were they working on?

If you consider blackmail as a tool, you have to have somewhere to insert the lever. I couldn't think where they could do this. Max wasn't married, so that wouldn't work – nobody to protect. He was head of his company, and having it off with a tart was hardly going to get him sacked or give us grounds to cancel the contract. It was the fact that they had used my ex-wife that intrigued me most, since it suggested something else, something more devious than a simple blackmail plot gone awry. I considered various notions about how the Russians might view Max being with my ex, but why would they care?

That's when it struck me. The connection between using my ex and the setup. Max was a decoy. They were after me all along. Of course they were. I was their gravy train, and without me the money would dry up instantly. People like Givens like to have something up their sleeve, and a connection like this between Max, the Russian gang, my wife and myself...well, that would do nicely to keep me in check if I got greedy, or came under pressure by Bannermann to do a deal to save my own skin. I suppose that's how Givens expects people to behave. He's probably right, because it is exactly what I would have done given half the chance, not that Bannermann is giving me any chance at all now.

The only thing is, the connection is not all that compelling as a blackmailing lever merely because my wife is a prostitute, although that would be pretty embarrassing. It does however become terribly compelling when my wife has murdered a man. Or appeared to have, because now I was beginning to think some very strange thoughts indeed. Was it possible that Givens had considered removing Max permanently? That Kelly had colluded with him, seduced me and lured me into the trap? Was Spang in on it, or better still, did he dream this up? It smells like his work, I have to say, but if so this is one chicken that really has come home to roost, because he's about to be visited by Bannermann, as are we all.

So, what really happened? Well, you're about to find out, but not from me, I assure you. By the way, if you're wondering why I'm telling you all this, pouring my heart out and incriminating myself, Givens, Spang and Kelly; all will become clear in time. I'm not in a position to explain right now, but let me be utterly clear just for the record: it isn't guilt, nor regret. What it is, well...you'll find out soon enough. That's all I have to say to you.

Just Like the Real Thing

I killed someone once.

God, I'm drunk. What time is it - no, don't tell me? It's still fucking light and I'm demi-glazed already. Anyway, ignore what I just said. Ah, fuck it, you are cute. I could jump you if I wasn't so pissed - I go both ways you know. Do you for nothing, I would. Do you like these - top man in the states did 'em, feels just like the real thing and the scars are tiny. Cost a few bob n'all, I can tell you. Gary – my other half – he paid for them. I only have to point 'em in his direction and he's drooling, tent pole and all. In some ways he's easy to please. In others, not so much. Just like Phillip, really. Men! They're all the same.

I can't believe he's dead. That bitch Dykeman called me, sounded fucking pleased with herself, the stuck up little cunt. Hung his stupid arse last night, they reckon. Too bad, since I wanted to kill him myself. Beat me to it. I really loved him you know, even though he was a right slimeball, but all politicians are, aren't they? All men, come to that. Just like a man, to run out on a girl, ain't it?

I don't know what's going to happen now. They picked up Gary and Sol already, so I heard. And Fred Smith, that dope-head off the Pullens. They must have gone to Phillip's, found him there. My turn next – she's leaving me till last, wants to see if I'll make a run for it. Pound to a penny they're watching me now – I'm sure they've been out there for days. You can feel it, the skin crawling eyes on you. The blokes all do it; strip you with their eyes because they wouldn't dare try that shit with their hands even while they're panting like dogs. Gutless.

Hung himself. I can't believe it.

Wonder how Miss Stuck-Up Andrea will take it? Fuck, I'd like to be there when they tell her. Prissy little tart, she is. Stuck up is right, like she's better than me, better than the other girls. Thinks she's special, the slag, but she ain't. She's no different, none of us are. Sure didn't look very special with a dead punter lying on top of her, that's for sure. And Phillip's face when he recognised her – that was a moment to treasure, I tell you. Now he knows what a tramp she really is, just another cheap opportunist after his money. He needed to know, needed to let go of the fucking illusion and see his wife for what she was. Never get over the bitch otherwise, although he did find another way to get free of her, didn't he?

But now he's lost me too, the dozy prat. I can't understand it. It was for him, you know, all for him. Wasted, all fucking wasted. Fucking typical. Why he married her in the first place is a fucking mystery too. He could have had any woman, someone proper; a real woman. Chose a simpering little slut from the suburbs with her frilly curtains and Habitat cushions. Cheap crap, cost a fortune. Cheap crap should be cheap, ain't that right? Look at these shoes – four hundred quid, no less. They do things for a girl's figure, shoes like this. Men can't get enough of them. The heels are real sharp, so they dig in to a bloke's chest lovely.

Men love that shit, I tell you. I know because when I started out, I worked for a tart who was into the domination line, and she was good at it. Taught me a lot, that one. All the good stuff, and I have to tell you it was fun, tying up the punters and giving them some stick – the cane was my fave. They were fucking pathetic, those creatures. Licking your arse and crawling around the flat on their knees. Humiliation; that's what they wanted and I tell you this – it's ever so easy to oblige, since they so fucking deserve it. The fact they pay you to do it to them just makes the whole deal sweet, it really does.

The other sort, the ones who want some submissive, gushing little tart like Sally, they're the hard ones to deal with. *Salubrious.* Don't make me laugh – her and her little tart's parlour. You can never tell about a punter when they first turn up: some are smart, some are ugly as fuck, but you find out soon enough. They want to tell you what to do, control you, call you filthy names, pay you to act cheap and dirty for them, because a real woman scares the shit out of them. They want you to pretend you are their little girl, so daddy can imagine what it's like to feel up his daughter, have his little princess suck him off, not that any of them would have the fucking nerve to actually do it for real, thank God.

Perverts, half of them queer but don't know it, the other half hating women and wanting revenge on us for something their mother did to them when they were six, some shit like that. Some of them want more than dirty talk. Some want to bend you over and spank you, others like a strap or a cane – Christ, that's painful. But the worst are the ones that like to knock you around. They get off on it, and it's how I lost my front teeth, not that you'd know since the implants are the best you can get. American again – what is it with this fucking country? The punter who knocked all my teeth out? A Polish sack of shit called Max.

I never believed my sister killed herself. She wasn't like that. She was younger than me – three years – and until I ran away I think she was shielded from the worst of it. After I left, the old man turned on her, and I always wondered what really happened, because Sylvie was a gobby little tart and she wouldn't have kept quiet about what was happening, I'm sure of it, not like I did. She wasn't scared of anything, least of all that old git.

Anyway, she was the only one of us who had the bust the wanker liked the look of. He was always complaining, humiliating me and my mother, bitching about how flat-chested all the women in his family were, how none of us were sexy and how we would never get a man with flat chests like ours. He used to tell us over and over how he wanted sons, how disappointing we were to him. We were nothing; nothing but trouble and costs, which he went on about all the fucking time. Cost of clothes. Cost of food. Cost of school, all the rest of it. We owed him, that's what he used to tell us, every fucking day. We owed him for being born, for being alive, for having him as a father. A debt we couldn't repay, not that it ever stopped him trying to collect, the fucking pervert.

Thing is, you have to understand that when Sylv started growing up, she got the boobs me and mum didn't have, and that's when dad started looking at her the same way he'd been looking at me for some time. And not just looking, of course. He was a right bastard, I can tell you. Funny enough though, when he got drunk he was much easier to handle – but don't take that too literal, like. I just mean he usually fell asleep as soon as he got home from the boozer, and his temper and his hands under the blankets would disappear for a night so we could all get some kip.

I still have trouble sleeping. I lie there, feeling scared although there's nothing to be scared of, like I'm waiting for something terrible to happen, something like a snake crawling up my leg and his smelly breath on my face. He never shaved much. I had big rashes on my neck where he scratched me but mum never said shit. She knew all along, the cow. Never said a fucking word; glad it was happening to me instead of her, I reckon. Fucking gutless bitch.

I ran away. Can you blame me? Thing is, I can't help feel some responsibility about my sister now, looking back. Would she still be alive if I hadn't run off? How the fuck can I tell, now it's too late? No going back, is there, Kelly?

No going forward now either, sweetie. Christ, this bottle is empty. Where's the new one...ah, here it is. Beefeater, love it. Proper gin at a sensible price, not like that posh Bombay shit. Better than drugs any day. C'mon Kelly, get the fucking top off, you tart. How tight did they do this up for Christ's sake? You're no weed, girl. Get a grip, Kelly; get a grip girl. Pretend it's a cock you're working with that grip of yours – eee, you should see the look on a man's face when I get my fingers wrapped tight around it. I have strong fingers; you can scare a punter half to death with a few sharp tweaks, I tell you.

After I left home, I didn't speak to anyone for a while. Next thing I hear, Sylvie was dead. Sleeping pill overdose, so they said. Never believed a word of it, me. Kelly can't be fooled, can she dear. Oh no, not me; I know the fucking score, I tell you. I know, learned it the hard way.

I was living in this bloke's flat in Clapham at the time. He was a prick, a stupid wanker who didn't know where he was going or why. Drugged up most of the time, and for a while there he got me on smack, which was the real low point of my life. He was the one started me on the streets, to pay for his habit. Beat me if I didn't get enough money, so of course I ended up robbing a bit to keep him off my back and keep my own habit going, and that's how I ended up in Pentonville for a while. The good thing was, that got me off the heroin.

Funny place to dry out, but there was this one woman, the dominatrix I told you about, and she looked after me, kept me away from the bad crowd who had the dope. For a price, like all things – keeping her satisfied. No free fucking lunches, right? I didn't mind though – with women she was nice enough, just gentle stuff, the usual between us girls. Not always gentle, exactly, but never the brutal stuff; she kept that for men. Learned a lot from her, Kelly did, didn't you sweetie. Kelly learned how to look after herself, how to deal with men and their pathetic needs, oh yes!

Bollocks. Run out of ice. Never mind, still plenty of tonic. Can do without that if I have to, just so long as I've got the gin. Always get your priorities right, that's what I say. My priority is me. Always has been, ever since I went on the game. I never minded it much, except when the punters started beating me. I hated that, but you find ways to get your own back, one way or another. It's all about keeping score; one punter knocks you about. Another one gets tied up and pays for it. And they love it;

the stricter you are with them, the harder you beat them, the more they'll cough up with the readies. Mistress Kelly; seems fair, don't it?

Swings and fucking roundabouts. I had all sorts; businessmen, actors, politicians, doctors, judges, old bill – you name it, they took it up the arse. I was doing well. Too well, actually, because we drew attention from the local crew, and that was how I met Gary.

Thing is, he wasn't like a pimp or anything. Not really. He was the local firm, and we were on his territory. He didn't come on all rough, threatening or anything. He just said we had to pay for his protection and although the woman who ran the flat was having none of it (she moved somewhere else in the end), he took me aside and offered to set me up on me own. He was nice to me, and wouldn't take a fuck as a bribe, which surprised me a bit. In the end, I jumped him for nothing, and it was the first time I think I ever enjoyed sex. It wasn't like he was that good at it. He just wasn't pervy. Didn't want to play games, didn't want to be submissive or dominant. He just seemed to like me, and when he touched me my skin didn't crawl, not like all the others.

We started going out, up west to see the shows, to the pictures or out for a meal. Gary knew all the good places and they knew him, so we always got good tables and free wine. I picked up right away that the bills didn't get paid all that often; sometimes they didn't even bother to give us one. That's when I realised that Gary was doing all right, although I wasn't stupid. Kelly isn't daft, are you my love? Oh no, I knew what was going on. He was respected because they were all afraid of him.

Then a strange thing happened. I had been to a nice dress shop with him and got a lovely frock really cheap, courtesy of the manager. Next time, I went there on my own. He tried to charge me full price so I mentioned Gary and the price was halved right off. This was what I really liked: they were afraid of me now because I was with Gary. That's when I decided it might be useful to get married.

It was Gary's idea to come off the game and set up the agency instead. Safe, better money, little risk. Smart move, and he introduced me to Sol – his solicitor – who told me the rules, how not to get in trouble with the bill. Of course, Gary took his cut, but I got the side benefits of being married to him, which meant my shopping sprees were wild from then on. He'd tell me where I could go, and I'd just drop his name to see them all shit themselves. Happy days, sweetie; happy fucking days.

After I had my tit job, Gary was so chuffed he decided we should have a holiday, just so he could show me off, I reckon. Believe it or not, I'd never been abroad. Didn't even have a passport. Anyway, we went on a cruise. Gary had bought four tickets, and given the other two away as a present to his mate Dan, who did a lot of work for Gary's team. Dan had just got married to this little chinky girl, quiet little thing called Ivy. Poison Ivy. I didn't mind, although I did think it was a bit weird going with them on their honeymoon, but what the fuck? We were going to the West Indies, and I was so up for it I would have gone with the entire West Ham football team – that's Gary's lot – *and* given 'em all a blowjob while I was at it.

On the third day, I wanted to go shopping and Dan wanted to get on dry land. Gary wasn't interested, said he would stay on board. Ivy was tired, so she said, so Dan and I went ashore. As it happened, I had forgotten my credit cards. Dan didn't have that much money on him, so I left him in a bar and popped back to the ship. I could hear that little cunt Ivy whining and groaning outside the cabin door, so I burst in and caught them at it.

It hadn't really occurred to me up till then that Gary would be fucking other women. I hadn't thought about it – being faithful is a weird thing to think about when you're a working girl, or been one. So Kelly surprised herself, didn't she? She was fucking furious, throwing things around and screaming, but Gary clamped his hand over my mouth right quick and reminded me where we was.

I wanted to get off the fucking boat and fly home right away, but Gary made me stay, took my cards and everything, so I couldn't go anywhere. Him and Ivy pleaded with me not to tell Dan. Ivy was crying like a stupid tart, but Gary promised me a diamond ring I'd seen in the jewellers and although I was fucking angry with him, my brains hadn't exactly fallen out. I kept my mouth shut, avoided Dan and Ivy – we ate in our cabin for the rest of the cruise.

I contented myself with giving Gary a very fucking hard time, and waited until we got back for the rest, to settle the bill properly with him. And with that tramp Ivy, make no mistake. No way I was going to let her get away with it. I did feel sorry for Dan though, didn't I? I did something later I regret, which doesn't happen to me much. Seeing how happy him and Ivy were, I whispered in Dan's ear one time, told him a little story about how his sweet little wife had been on the game before he met her. He didn't say nothing, but he looked really hurt. Still, she deserved it and I'm not sad she's dead, neither, considering what she cost me.

We split up when we got back, Gary and I, but not for all that long. We had too much business going on, and I liked hammering the credit cards too much to do without him; he could afford it, no problem. Him and Spang were making a mint, in partnership with our Councillor Goodhall. I met him a couple of times, and he was quite a looker, wasn't he? Very smooth, intelligent sort. Had a simpering wife – that Andrea – but a nice house.

Of course he came on to me, in a sort of offhand way, probably because he was shit-scared of Gary like everyone else. But I picked up the clues, and turned up at his house one afternoon in me best tart's drawers, heels and a skirt slit up to me neck. He took one look and dropped his pants, drooling like a dog in heat.

Thing is, I fancied him a bit, but that wasn't why I was after him. I wanted to pay Gary back, and fucking Phillip was the way to really get him pissed. Not so pissed he could do anything about it though, because Phillip had all the contracts, controlled all the money. Without him, Gary and Spang were fucked, and I knew it. Sweet, eh? Nothing riles Gary more than being powerless, believe you me. That's why he won't let me tie him up, see.

Phillip really fancied himself, but I have to admit he wasn't half bad in bed. Better than Gary – better than anyone I'd had, I reckon. He made me come so many times I lost count, but the funny thing is he didn't believe it. He thought I was faking it, and I couldn't do nothing about it.

It's a bit embarrassing to admit why this was, but this one time I did a little film with another girl and this African stud, a boxer called Lenny Lumbago. He got called that because of his back trouble, which he reckoned he got in the ring, but it ain't true. He got it that afternoon from having me and the other girl hanging off him like Christmas tree lights. Did his back in, we did, poor bastard.

After, we were all sitting around having a drink and watching the playback. It looked alright, really. Lenny was giving it to me right proper and I was getting off on it, you could see that. Thing is, we all started giggling, because there was this funny noise. Took me a few minutes to work out it was me: I sounded like a squeaky speaking clock or something. It's so fucking strange, hearing yourself like that. I had no idea that's what I sounded like when I was getting off, but it did explain why Phillip was so suspicious.

Explained a few things, actually: it isn't the sound of love, it's the sound of fear and hate and pain, turned into animal sounds of sex. Have I always made this sound? Is this what he taught me? To fake the sounds so he'd think I was enjoying it? No wonder the old man used to put his hand over my mouth to shut me up. I always thought it was so mum wouldn't hear.

Poor old Phillip: what made me laugh was that he was so offended each time I got off and he thought I was faking it, so he kept trying harder and harder, and every time he did I got off more than before. As tricks go, every girl should learn this one, 'cos it sure makes a man work that bit harder, and for longer.

Now, you're not going to believe this, but *I* know, don't I? See; I fell in love with Phillip. Fuck you if you don't believe it, but it's true. Why would I lie about it? There was just something about him, something he had that Gary didn't. He could be gentle, like no bloke I'd met. He used to brush my hair. His hands on me didn't feel dirty, they felt warm and loving. Yes Kelly, that's it. You can say it: loving. I felt like Phillip was loving me instead of fucking me. Never thought that before.

Did I want more? Is the Pope a catholic? Did I want Gary to find out, now I was feeling different about it? No fucking way. This was a good thing, and my little revenge seemed stupid in comparison.

You can't keep secrets, can you girl? Big fucking mouth I have, don't I? Got really pissed one night, had a huge row with the cunt, told him I was fucking his business partner. He looked stunned, like I'd just tasered him.

'With Spang?' he said, the idiot. 'No, you fuckwit. With Phillip.'

Bugger, there it was. Could have stuck with Spang, just for the wind-up. But no chance: as soon as the words were out of my mouth, I knew I'd fucked everything up. Stupid Kelly, just like always. Got a good thing going? Kelly will fuck it up, won't you girl?

I had to do some serious tit-jiggling to get Gary's mind off what I'd told him, but I knew it was just a matter of time. I thought there would be trouble, but not the kind that showed up, I can tell you.

I didn't see Gary for a couple of days after that. Or Phillip. Just kept my head down, waiting. Then Gary came home and sat down opposite me in the kitchen. In a very quiet voice – scary because it was so quiet, you know how *that* is – he told me he didn't care about Goodhall, and that I could actually help him if I kept seeing Phillip. I'm not fucking stupid. There was a price, and this was part of it. I knew that, didn't I? That's when Gary told me about Max.

Thing is, Gary couldn't possibly have known it was Max who knocked all my teeth out. Actually, Gaz took some stick over that, because when people saw me all bruised and fucked up they thought he did it, what with his rep and all. Unfair, really; in all our time together, he's never laid a hand on me. No; when Gary wanted to punish me he hit me where it really hurt – he'd cancel my cards or refuse to pay the bill. I like a shrewd man.

I was lost for words, so I just sat there. Funny ain't it, how if you don't say nothing, men have to keep talking. So Gary started prattling on about Max, how he was fucking up some deal they'd cooked up, how much money they were losing. 'How much is it worth to you to sort this out?' I asked. He looked funny at me, and said 'Fixing this problem is worth ten grand of anyone's money'. We left it at that, but we understood each other. Oh yes. We understood all right.

I thought about the ten grand a lot. Even at four hundred a pop, a girl can get a lot of shoes for that kind of cash, know what I mean? I didn't really have a plan though, not until Gary gave me a little push in the right direction. He mentioned Sally, who I'd forgotten about, and her tart's parlour down the road. He was cunning, was Gary; put the thought in my head how it would look if people knew Phillip's wife was whoring with a Russian crook.

That's what Gary was after then – a way to keep Phillip in check. I could use that too, don't think that didn't occur to me.

And don't think it didn't occur to me that I might be able to pay Max back for what he'd done to me, as well as stuff up that stupid little tart Andrea. Phillip kept pining after her – God knows why – and I knew how to break him out of it, no trouble. A couple of nice pictures with the faces nice and clear, and Phillip would stop thinking about Andi and think more about me instead. With all my experience, I could give him plenty to think about, keep him well occupied.

I don't know why I talked to Phillip about it before hand. No, I do – it was to check what Gary had told me. Wish I hadn't, somehow; maybe he'd still be alive, like my sister, isn't that right? Who the fuck knows? I did mention it to him – the general idea, not his wife's part in it – and I don't mind telling you I was disappointed when he caught on, and seemed to like the idea. I dunno – I guess I wanted him not to be like the others, to be different somehow. Stupid, really, because they really are all the fucking same, ain't that right?

Why the fuck Gary gave him the knife is a mystery to me. We got it arranged so that Gary would send Max a present – some little thing – and a phone number so he could get another present; me and Sally. But the knife – I really wonder about it. Max rings up in due course – he'd used the agency before and two other girls had suffered for it – and I wondered for a minute if he would recognise my voice – I don't usually work the phones – because I did his, the second he started speaking.

I went all dizzy for a minute, thought I might blow it, but he was chatting away all to himself and didn't notice. I got my breath back, told him that Mr. Givens has arranged a little entertainment, and that I could send a car to pick him up on the day, which he liked the sound of, apparently. I didn't tell him I would be driving the car.

I'm sure he recognised me straight away, but he still got in the car. I did my best to smile at him, showing my new teeth. He made a few comments as we drove, along the lines of being pleased to see me again, so he knew all right. On the spur of the moment, I told him that the other girl he would meet liked the rough stuff, more than me. I was there for other things, I told him suggestively, and he lapped it up. 'She likes it?' he said, leering. I nodded, feeling a bit bad about it, but a plan's a plan, ain't it?

So we arrive at Sally's, and we go in through the back door, have a few drinks and I spike Sally's with some gear I got off Freddy. On impulse, I also put some in Max's glass as well – not a planned thing, just spur of the moment. The stuff was supposed to be a date-rape drug like GBH, but I think Freddy fucked up because Sally passed out instead of just being dozy and helpless. Max though - he was made of stronger stuff – or maybe I just didn't give him enough.

I was sitting on the couch. They were on the floor, with Max on top of Sylvie. I was a bit pissed, not as much as I am now, but not out of control, at least, I didn't think so. I was just sitting there, watching and waiting, ready to get the little camera out that Gary had given me, but mostly I was thinking about what I could do when the old man started getting woozy. I couldn't make up my mind. I just kept looking at the knife, which he had showed us both earlier: he'd been waving it about, calling it his famous sword! What the fuck? It was lying on the table where he'd left it when me and Sylvie started doing a little lesbo show. What kind of pervert would want to see that, sisters doing each other? I looked up from the knife when I heard something that made my blood run cold, that same whimpering sound I make, and there he was, leaning back and punching Sylvie. She was incapable of fighting him off, just like I'd been, nearly out cold with his hard hand clamped over my mouth, her mouth, can't breathe, can't scream, can't get away. I saw his fists going like pistons, I remembered them so well; hard and fast like a machine, blood on his knuckles, blood from her mouth, from her nose – broken now – Sylvie's blood, my blood, it all looks the same as it runs down your face, hot and sticky and strange tasting. I can't help her, sitting there paralysed with fear and anger. It's me lying there, me taking it: me, a little girl who knew fuck all about the world, about sex or anything. I trusted him, I tried to love him; he was my fucking father, wasn't he? I knew it was wrong, what he was doing. I tried to stop him, I really did, I tried and cried but he just punched me like he's punching my sister now because I wasn't there to protect her. She was helpless too, like I was before when it was my turn. Her turn now, the poor cow, her turn because I ran away. I couldn't help her. I didn't run out on her but she died anyway. It wasn't my fault, was it? There was nothing I could do. Or was there? I was able to fight back, wasn't I? I'm a big girl now, daddy, and I know what to do about scum like you. I've learned the hard lesson daddy. Now it's your turn. I'm coming Sylv...hold on... I'm going to rescue you, save you from this, I swear it. Here I come, I've got this knife Sylvie, the knife Gary gave me. I've unfolded it carefully from the ivory handle with its brass studs so I don't cut myself on it, all shiny and sharp like the one he used to hold to my neck when I wouldn't suck his filthy fucking lollipop. Now I'm walking over, I'm coming to save you Sylvie. Daddy looks up over his shoulder, grinning at me. I have to stop him grinning. I have to stop him, get him away from Sylvie or she will die, over and over again. Have to: I'm behind him now, looking down at him humping away and now he's frozen in mid-fuck, the knife is stuck in his side really hard, right between the ribs, grinding on the bone, and into his grinning evil heart. That's wiped the fucking grin off his stupid face. I knew he was dead even before he dropped, and I hope he did too, the grinning evil cunt.

God, what have I done?

I sat there for a while. I wasn't shocked. I was pleased. He deserved it. I never gave the tart a second thought, until it struck me that Phillip should see this. I needed help, and he was the first person I thought of, so I called him. He didn't want to come over, of course, but I persuaded him right enough. A bit later he turned up, all pale and shitting himself. When he saw the body, he was shaky but didn't back off. When he saw who the tart was, that's when he lost it – puking all over the kitchen. Men!

Spang sorted it all out. I knew he would. I'd worked it out beforehand; Sally would cop the blame. I knew I'd get away with it. What I didn't know about was the fucking webcam, and it cost me a lot more than ten grand to find that out. It cost me everything.

Mysterious Ways

Please, make yourself comfortable.

I have quite a story to tell you; how I came to be the best fundraiser in the borough; how the church was saved; how the Lord has set me a test I cannot fathom; how I'm implicated in a crime I had no knowledge of; how I came to hold damning evidence against some of the most culpable people in my parish; how a young man faced a terrible choice, and a deathbed promise I made. Things like that. But mostly, I want to tell you about a remarkable woman called Ivy, who I had the privilege of getting to know quite well. She cannot speak for herself, so I will speak for her. She would have wanted that.

Where to start? The modern trend is to jump in, start in the middle of a story and work backwards and forward simultaneously. I'm not terribly modern – how could I be, given my vocation? You don't don the cloth if you want to be a part of the glittering world, all high-speed and instant everything. The vacuum of modernity, a cold place without a heart, it seems. No place for the spirit of man, not any more. No place for me, really.

I'm sorry, I sound rather self-pitying, do I not? I'll stop doing that...sorry, I'm laughing now because I was about to say something rather unlikely. I was about to assure you I would be truthful too, but of course that's ridiculous isn't it? Have you ever met anyone who prefaced remarks with the admission: 'of course, I *will* lie a bit'. It's like that joke about the politician who, when challenged, replies 'of course I'm lying, but hear me out'. I've met many characters in my time, some of them quite reprehensible to be frank, and none have ever presented themselves as anything less than honest, reliable, stout fellows.

I hear the most appalling stories from them – confessions, of course, because amongst the irreligious there is some confusion between the Catholic confessional and the Anglican pastoral. It doesn't matter; I just listen to anyone who seeks me out. It is, after all, what I'm paid to do. Save souls, if I can, for there is no limit to the forgiveness of the Lord – although I have to admit mine is tested from time to time. I hope he looks on poor Phillip Goodhall with his kindly light. That's a terrible thing, to take one's own life. Poor man. Poor, *poor* man; another one that got away, I'm afraid.

They all get away in the end.

Many of us - those who are called – we wonder if we are not much more than an anachronism in these modern days. It's a natural enough thought. We make so little impact on so much poverty, literal *and* spiritual. I've worked so hard for many years – I'm sorry if that sounds self-aggrandising – I just mean I've made the effort, but the results are negligible. I don't believe I've made any real impact on the parish, done any good. I'm not sure they even notice me, and if they do they treat me with suspicion.

It is a strange world in which those with humble purpose and good intent are so vilified and distrusted, but you cannot blame people for this. They have been lied to, misled, betrayed and cheated over and over again, all through history, first by their feudal masters, the aristocracy and the church, then politicians and finally, the corporations. Now they can get this history of betrayal on their computers, and they can read it, understand it too. They talk among themselves, fanning their just disaffections.

They have educations circumscribed by politics and class, so they are not equipped to deal with the complexities. Inevitably, the nuance is lost along with the trust, and with it goes discrimination – not the racial kind – I mean the kind that can still tell good from bad. In that situation, everything is bad until proven good, guilty until proven innocent.

No more, the implicit trust for authority, the respect for it. All authority is suspect: why do you think they beat up nurses, teachers, police or firemen? They can read the papers, watch TV, listen to the radio, search the web. The deceit is exposed and nobody is really fooled any more. Yet they can do nothing about it but get angrier and angrier.

These are testing times, although that is obviously true of all times, past and present. Future too, I have little doubt. It's all one long struggle, one long test, or so it would appear. Dear me, could we not have had it a little easier, Lord? Just a bit? But no: God does like to set His little tests, as you will see.

The consequence of all this is that people round here remain tribal and defensive, and hostile to the church. I cannot seem to reach them. I do get some modest response from younger people, but only because we share a curious and somewhat ironic interest in violence. I used to box when I was younger, and I have a few trophies to show for it - Lord, let me not indulge in too much sinful pride – but young men, and more than a few girls I must say, they took an interest from time to time and we run a club for them where they can learn some skills, get some exercise, channel some of their aggression.

But that's about it, I'm afraid. I always believed one should earn respect, and I knew when they sent me here it would be tough, but I was young and resilient, full of Christ's loving fire and warming brimstone. I was up for a fight once more, the good fight, God's fight, but there was nothing to hit, no target to aim at. Just an empty, decaying church with graffiti all over it and pools of water in the corner of the nave. I hope it was water.

I don't know. I expect I sound naive to you, but I don't mind. To have any idealism left after twenty years serving this parish merits a tiny, modest amount of pride – I'm sure that isn't too sinful, is it? I am more certain about the spiritual dimension to my work than the temporal. It is in what people sometimes refer to as 'the real world' – as if I don't live there too – that I find it difficult to reconcile my faith with my actions. I'll come back to this, if you don't mind.

It's where the church and money meet, that's where the problem lies – and always has, I expect. *This* is the real world, isn't it? Money talks, and it speaks the language of the gutter a lot of the time. You know, when I was at Cambridge, we had a tutor who was the nicest, sweetest, most devout little old man imaginable. One day, he told us we had to be prepared for the kind of people we were likely to be working with because, unprepared, some incumbents were so shocked by the language of the street they gave up on the spot and resigned. Too many, apparently, so they decided to give us a taste of what was to come.

I cannot tell you how shocking it was when this dear old man started swearing at us. There was no profanity he didn't know, nor use with a venom I could not believe was contained in such a frail body. One chap in my class near passed out, that's how shocking it was. The tutor continued this tirade for half an hour, picking on us at random and expecting level, sober responses no matter how outrageous he was. I can't possibly bring myself to give you any examples, but the F word and the C word featured heavily, as did numerous sexual acts, all of which are utterly loathsome. Most of them I hadn't even heard of, although I did look them up afterwards just for the sake of completeness. Honestly.

I'm being facetious. I apologise. I'm not terribly good at the confessional myself. More of an internaliser, wrestling in private with my soul kind of chap. Rather British, actually; stiff upper lip, is it not? And perhaps I'm just procrastinating, trying to delay talking about the money, and the trouble it's got me into. We never learn, do we Lord? Why did you make us in such poor fashion, so uncomprehending of Your Divine Will most of the time? And what kind of useful test can You apply to such defective products, created out of this sodden clay from which You decided to form us? Did you run out of decent materials by day six?

The church always seems to be swimming in money, but that's only because we can put on a good show like everyone else. More front than Herod's, as we used to say at college. Centuries of practice, although the papists put us to shame every time. They've got their own city-state, for God's sake! Islam has Mecca. We've got Lambeth Palace. Not quite the same, is it? Lord, I sound jealous.

What people do not consider is how much it costs to maintain a vast legacy of old buildings. Another issue I have with my maker is gravity. Why could he not have made an exemption for churches, so they wouldn't fall down all the time? It's no wonder we get caught up in corruption and scheming.

Christianity is an expensive business to run, mark my words. The fact we made it that way by being so ostentatious about our places of worship, so keen to humble the common man in the face of overwhelming grandeur, only suggests we got rather carried away with our self-importance. It is not an easy circle to square, Christ's asceticism and the wealth of the church. All that port and chateaubriand. Glorious vicarages with lofty, elegant rooms whose heating bills could finance a home for orphans.

Still, my faith does not depend on such paradoxes, nor am I deterred by them. There are many things to change, but one thing at a time – that's the humble way. Anything else, and you're up to your necks in politics and end up looking like my church does now; bitter, divided, intolerant, irrelevant. As ye sow...

You know, I often wonder why they didn't teach us marketing along with swearing. When I came here, my efforts – looking back on it – were just pathetic. Orange day-glo posters asking for donations. Leaflets larded with fatuous pieties, badly printed on cheap paper I kept finding in the bin for months after they went out. People brought them here just to throw them away, some kind of insult. Or a demonstration of their contempt.

If we were a business, the church would have gone into administration long ago. As it is, we're rich enough to bumble on for another century or so, enough time to completely undermine Christ's word through our contradictory actions, our hypocrisy and our ineffectuality. We could do good, you know. Make a difference, a contribution. There's nothing wrong with the Christian ethos. It's kind and modest and generous. What's wrong with Christianity is us – Christians – and the way we practice our faith with so little reverence for its teachings.

People know this. I had no flock to speak of when I came here. It was the usual thing: middle-aged people and older. The older generations died off. The middle-aged got old. There was no-one behind them, nobody new coming through the door. We were dying, and so were the contributions.

Not long after I took residence, I had a local firm in to assess the state of the properties. The things they found really shocked me. I spoke to the bishop and he shrugged his shoulders before getting into his chauffeur-driven limo to go to lunch at Claridges in Mayfair. Perhaps it is true I lost hope at that time. I feel ashamed to admit it, but Christ understands my weakness and forgives me. All part of the test, isn't that right? We are nothing without we are tested, apparently.

Will it sound too pious if I say my prayers – my fervent, desperate, endless prayers – were answered, admittedly after rather a long delay? I know it's just a way of saying it, but I should be consistent, surely?

However you want to describe it, one morning after several years in which I'd bumbled along scraping together what I could, I went to open the main doors and remembered I hadn't looked in the contributions box for a while –hardly much incentive to do so, really. I unlocked it and there were two envelopes inside, each containing a bank draft for two thousand pounds, made out to the church fund. A week later, there was another one, for a larger amount. I have been receiving these cheques irregularly ever since, the last one recently. And it was the last one ever, as I will explain, assuming I ever get there – I am taking my time here, sorry about that.

The relationship between the church and donations is rather obscure. We tend not to ask questions, frankly. It is too inconvenient when you have to give the money back. We do have a sense of propriety, however. Most of us – the majority actually. I'm not *that* disillusioned and nor is my church.

I did the right thing and rang the bank the cheque was drawn on. They wouldn't tell me anything. I got an appointment with the manager when the next one arrived – I still hadn't banked the others – and he was unctuous and vague, an attempt at polite dismissal that didn't quite come off, and didn't suit him much if you ask me. He did tell me one thing though; the money was coming from a reliable source.

'It's not the proceeds of crime, if that's what you're afraid of,' he told me. I talked to my bishop and afterwards, I banked the cheques. I called the builders and they started work. I have kept them fully employed pretty much ever since.

Once the church work was underway, I had enough to start rebuilding the youth club. That had been shut for many years, but in twelve months we had restored the fabric of the building, and the following year we started up the boxing club. I had help for the first time – the local community do like their boxing and they have a few professionals still living here, who willingly pitched in once they discovered they could go a few rounds with a tricky vicar. We had some good fun, actually. It was the first time I felt I had earned their respect, just for the wrong damn thing.

To cut a long story short, I have raised so much money I've redecorated the church itself, replaced all the old pews that had rotted, fitted out the club and bought a 12-seater van to ferry our pensioners back and forth. No other church in the borough has raised as much, and certainly not from a single source, for no other funds of any real size have ever come this way. We produce a glossy newsletter, run an excellent website and finance all sorts of outreach programs in the community – soup kitchens, drug treatment programs and a needle exchange (my, that got me in hot water), battered wives, homeless people – all kinds of things, all of them the Lord's honest work and not a bible or a prayer in sight.

This is the problem – theoretically, at least; if I attach the slightest whiff of faith into any of it, the thing fails. I take comfort in the fact of the work and its efficacy. That the propaganda fails is neither here nor there, since I never was a proselytiser. It is not the faith itself that is virtuous; it is the works produced by that faith and in its name. Converts are akin to a strange kind of greed among too many of my brethren, like a lust for sheer numerical superiority. Quality, not quantity, I believe.

Speaking of quality, you can't attribute much to a storyteller who promises to tell you about Ivy and so steadfastly manages not to do so. I cannot obfuscate any longer however, so here she is.

I first met her one night in the church. It was late – I was fixing some lights I think – and I went to lock up. At the last moment, I noticed a head just above the top of the pews, else I would have locked her in for the night. I went over and there she was, an elegant Chinese miniature like a porcelain doll, a child-woman with tears running down her face, knees drawn up to her chest in a little foetal ball. Her legs were bleeding from cuts made with a strap by the look of it. One eye was all puffy.

I sat down next to her, asked nothing – which is often the best way – and said a little prayer for her out loud, asking Jesus to look after this frail woman in her time of need. To my astonishment, she giggled and stopped crying. 'I'm not very frail, father,' she told me, and I had to believe her, such was the determined look she gave me. Her tears were of pain, not self-pity.

We talked for hours. She told me all about her life, her background, how hard things had been for her. She was so candid, so proud that she had made it so far against such appalling odds, and she believed that God would rescue her one day if she earned His respect.

What a woman! I'd never heard anything so passionate, so compelling and so moral. She had never succumbed to drugs, never resorted to selling herself, never missed a day's work or complained about her lot. She was incorruptible, but without the slightest sanctimony or self-righteousness. It was simply how she was; absolutely uncompromising in the face of duress that you or I might crumple under in a moment...oh dear, *I'm so sorry*. That was horribly patronising of me, unforgivably presumptuous. I have no idea what you might do. I speak only of my own weakness and I have no right to assuage it by dragging you down to my level for company. I apologise.

Ivy was an example to me, right from the off. She was so candid I opened my heart to her about all the worries I had, and of course it ended up with her comforting me, the blood still trickling down her legs now and then. I did wash them and treat them before she went home: please do not get the impression I was that self-absorbed. She just overpowered me for a while, drew me out with such sympathy and warmth I couldn't help myself. She wanted to comfort me, and she really did. Remarkable, generous, tough woman.

We did all kinds of things together, Ivy and I. She did unpaid secretarial work, not just for me but others, like the wardens for example. She kept the books (she was good with computers, although for the life of me I have no idea where she learned), wrote hilarious letters I had to discretely correct, her written English not being quite as accurate as I think she might have liked. She cleaned for me often, as it's very difficult to keep good people here even though we pay well. I think it's because the buildings are so hard to work in.

She also did audition for the choir, but the choirmaster couldn't stand her reedy, high-pitched voice, which he compared to an unbearable Chinese instrument of torture. No sense of pitch, he told me. It didn't matter, to me or to Ivy, I suspect. I enjoyed her company very much, partly because she was reassuring, a symbol of something good and, dare I say this? – pure. Yes: Ivy was a pure woman. That's what makes the whole thing so utterly inscrutable, to coin a phrase. You see for yourself.

The other part I played in Ivy's life was ambiguous to me. I have never quite known what to make of it, good or bad – or even if it really had much to do with me at all. It is the matter of her marriage, and that she met her prospective husband through the church. His name is Dan, and he's under arrest now for Ivy's murder, so you can imagine my concern, surely?

I suppose I did start things off. Dan had been working here, helping me set up the boxing club because he was an ex-pro corner-man, a good one judging by some of his work that I saw when I went to a few fights, which I enjoy from time to time, if for no other reason than I don't go in mufti, but wear the collar just to see the amazed looks and bafflement on the part of my fellow enthusiasts. It's quite amusing in an innocent way, or at least I hope it is.

I noticed right off that Dan was taking an interest in Ivy, from a distance. They didn't speak to each other as far as I'm aware, but Dan started hanging around the church for no apparent reason, looking for work rather than having to be asked. It seemed rather too good to be true, so I didn't object. These were hard times and it was all hands to the pumps, if you know what I mean. I also knew a bit about Dan, and what I heard was not at all good. He was a very troubled soul indeed, and having him under God's roof seemed appropriate.

After a while, he realised he'd given the game away and asked me about Ivy. I told him a few things, and without really thinking what I was doing I became rather indiscrete. It was impulsive, and the way it turned out it was just as well, which is an object lesson in something or other, but quite what I haven't identified yet, although the phrase 'works in mysterious ways' might easily come into it, given my vocation and temperament. It is a most convenient catch-all for the severely challenged, the sorely tested.

What I told him was that Ivy was an indentured servant. She was heavily in debt and had been all her adult life, with no chance of ever earning enough to pay back the gang that owned the debt. I had no idea how much money Dan had; he was never flashy, never donated, bought his round but expected you to buy yours. I only learned this when he came to me one day and told me he had freed Ivy from her bond, bought it himself. How he came to do this I did not dare ask, since I knew the kind of people he worked with. But it was true; Ivy was free.

Dan and Ivy married six months later. I conducted the service. Whatever doubts I had about the unlikely pairing were instantly dismissed when I saw them together. He was doting, child-like, docile. She was fun, haughty and wilful, then contrite and obedient. And they laughed all the time as they played their roles, him the dull fool always at her mercy, she the relentless tease who did it to hide how much she loved him. It was truly beautiful to watch.

I hope I've summed that up accurately, because my intention is to contrast that relationship with the notion that this same man, this same committed, loving spouse, could deliberately poison his wife, slowly and premeditatedly over a period of weeks. I cannot bring myself to believe it, but I understand he has confessed to exactly this.

I feel a terrible despair when I consider it, consider the possibility. It is possible, given his nature, but how could it have happened? What could bring about such a change? I have to agree with Detective Bannermann. She was the one who told me about it, and she believed Dan was making up the story to offset the terrible pain of his loss. I find this far more credible, but my sorrow for Dan remains just as overwhelming, and I cannot entirely free myself from a sense of guilt.

I visited Ivy many times during her illness. This is part of my work, and my faith does shield me from an excess of melancholy. I am saddened to see the light dim, but because I have faith that a good soul will find a place in eternity, my burden is eased a little. I know that sounds suspiciously convenient, but that's how faith is supposed to work. It should help us at dark times, for if it does not, what use is it? Do not mistake me; faith is not a crutch, it is a framework. Only by the discipline of applying it to every waking hour of every day does one gain strength. Faith without application is worse than useless, for it always fails us at the testing time.

I sat with Ivy for many hours. I held her hand as I read to her, told her about what we were doing, how the kids in the club were getting on. She got weaker, but kept smiling as best she could. There was little pain that I could detect; it was more like she was just fading away from us, life draining out of her as if some plug in her soul had been dislodged. Dan was terribly distraught, but I'm not certain now if I read it correctly. At the time, I thought it was sorrow troubling him, but looking back in light of what's happened, I must concede it might have been conflict. It is very troubling, and I suspect it will remain that way.

Towards the end, Dan could hardly bear to be in the room. He would sit in the lounge, an untouched drink in front of him, staring at the wall. Waiting like a stone, a statue that wept. The last time I saw Ivy alive, she must have known it was time. She had a strange look about her, fiery and defiant. As Dan shut the door behind him to resume his vigil, she took my hand and pulled me close to her. In a soft whisper, she spoke for nearly an hour without a single interruption. I tried to speak a couple of times early on, but she stopped me. 'What I do not tell you now, I will never tell at all,' she said, grave and direct. Chastened, I remained silent until she stopped speaking.

When she had finished, she looked at me, eyes kind and sparkling. 'It is up to you now, Roger.' She never called me Roger before and I started to cry. She smiled. 'Have faith, my son, have faith and you will be saved. Go to my dresser and look in the middle drawer.' I pulled back – somehow she was holding my head to her breast and I'd made her gown wet – and did as she said. There was a heavy manila envelope in the drawer. I took it out and turned to Ivy. 'What is it?'

She motioned me back. Her voice was fading. 'Do not look now. Later, Roger, later. Do you promise to do what I have asked?'

I nodded. '*Say it!*' she demanded, hissing at me. I pulled back. 'I swear I will do as you ask, Ivy, so long as no laws are broken. My promise is conditional on what this envelope contains. If you want my unconditional word, I must see what is in here'.

Ivy shook her head. 'I trust you, and I trust you will know what to do. I need nothing more from you except your love and your forgiveness.'

That's when I started crying again, and I'm not even slightly ashamed to admit it. What man would not shed tears when deeply moved by the glory of God, a man whose soul has yet been touched by His exceedingly strange sense of humour?

I said earlier I'm introspective. I struggle within, not without. For weeks I wrestled with my conscience, back and forth like Jesus in the desert. In the end, I came to the conclusion that there were two separate elements to my dilemma, and the promise I had made only applied to one of them. This might be a little bit of sophistry on my part, but I can live with it. Apparently, God can too, because this time he answered my prayers with alacrity.

One issue was this: the contents of the envelope. This was a vast amount of material Ivy had collected, hacked or generally stolen, and all of it was, she assured me, utterly damning of a whole group of people. She said it was up to me what I did with it. I am not a policeman. I should not judge. I simply didn't know what to do, so I prayed. The other matter, and my promise, was something I could defer for now, since the two problems were not connected. Not entirely, anyway. I sound equivocal now, and I don't mean to. It's just that they could be addressed independently.

You see my problem? To put it crudely, was I prepared to be a grass? Was that my job, my role? Is that what vicars do? I was thinking this very thing when there was a knock on the office door. It was a young man called Viktor, who trained at the club, an excellent boxer and a nice young man, polite and intelligent. Superb control in the ring; he got it from doing martial arts, so he said. He was going to show me some moves but we never got around to it.

I hadn't seen him for a long time. He looked very distraught. He handed me a DVD and tried to tell me something, but he choked on his words. I sat him down and put on the kettle. While I busied myself making some tea, he managed to tell me that he had obtained a laptop computer from the house where a murder took place. This was a famous case in the locality, a man called Max who was stabbed to death by a prostitute. What I didn't know until that moment was that Max was Viktor's father.

I was shocked. I had no idea, of course I didn't. Nobody did, it seemed. I asked him about the laptop, why he'd told me, and what was on the DVD? He looked grim and resolved. 'It is the murder of my father. The people who did it. It is the most horrible thing, ever.'

Apparently, the prostitute Sally – who I knew as Andrea Goodhall – turned on the webcam built into the laptop before the assault took place, but didn't save the recording, so it was lost.

However, Viktor – who is good at this kind of thing – he realised that the temporary file might still exist, and he recovered it using some technical magic or other. I think I got that right.

I have watched the DVD. It is difficult to bring myself to describe what is on it. Suffice to say, it is a film of a man being murdered in the most brutal of circumstances by one woman. Another – Andrea – is beaten up. As well as these three people, two others appear at the scene and are compellingly implicated in the crime, one of which is Phillip Goodhall, the other his solicitor. Phillip must have known this DVD existed, and killed himself rather than face the shame.

I pity him. I do not pity the others, and since they were all implicated in numerous crimes by the materials Ivy gave me as well, I took Viktor's DVD as a sign, my prayer answered, and decided to hand both over to Bannermann, who Viktor had arranged to meet, but changed his mind at the last moment. Sorely troubled, he came to me instead.

This change of mind was understandable, because I have to tell you something about Viktor, something very brave and difficult for him. Viktor idolised his father, but the man was a woman-beater. Viktor knew this all along, but somehow he'd suppressed the memories of his mother being beaten, hidden them away in the dark somewhere. I think that he also came to believe stories about his father that could not possibly be true: how he was a fighter pilot in the war, for example. Max was too young for that, but Viktor seemed to believe it unquestioningly, perhaps creating a myth to obscure the reality he couldn't live with.

Now, seeing the film, the full force of those memories had been released in the most violent and uncompromising way. What an awful experience that must have been, watching his father be murdered, at the same time confronting a terrible truth about the man he loved so much. What I found remarkable was how he faced his awful revelation, how brave he was to give me the disk. He called it a betrayal of his father's memory. I told him his actions honoured his father through the bravery and honesty of his son.

I don't know how much that helped, but the Mercedes he stole from Gary Givens seems to be some modest kind of compensation. He told me about that too, and it cheered him up a little – and me, to be honest. That's one crime I won't be reporting any time soon, nor the inadvertent part I played in it.

The principles in the murder, with the exception of Goodhall, have all been arrested now. Along with poor old Dan: what a shame.

My promise then. Ivy told me something, confessed something, that has shaken my faith to the core, since there is a paradox I am confronted with I have no idea how to resolve. This is what she told me.

The envelope contained materials that Ivy had collected over the years. She was outraged at the behaviour of those around her, and she had been sorely abused by Gary Givens during her honeymoon, when she and Dan went on a cruise with Givens and his wife. It was, she told me, the only thing she was really ashamed of. She didn't explain the circumstances, but I understood full well that the subject was now revenge. I suppose that's how it started, but as she told it, a kind of righteous anger overtook her, even as she lay there on the pillow.

After the cruise, she started digging through old files, visiting archives, burrowing through computer records. As she uncovered more and more corruption, the bigger grew the file. She told me she had no idea what she was going to do with it all at first. But then she had a good idea, and this is where I get into trouble.

Ivy Cheng was my benefactor. Over a number of years, she had personally donated more than a quarter of a million pounds, and she got the money by blackmailing all the criminals she had gathered information on. She had established a steady stream of illicit money, extracted from people she hated. She gave it all to the church, and after she told me of its provenance, *she made me promise to keep it.*

So there it is then. All this time, I've rebuilt the church and done all these good works, funded by the proceeds of crime after all. But whose crime? Ivy, for extracting the money? Isn't she acting as God's tax collector: from the proceeds of crime, even God takes his cut. Ivy Cheng: the Chinese Robin Hood? Is that just sophistry, clever words disguising criminal intent? Whose money was it by the time it fell into the donations box?

Seriously, I am completely baffled by the morality of all this. How am I supposed to know what is right; here, outside of temporal law. We all live under God's law, and Thy Will Be Done. Is this His will? As my profane instructor would have put it – fucked if I know! Damn! I enjoyed that; I'll do the abject penance later on. Profanity or no, it is His will? I have to think it is, since it's all so damn well done. Nobody knows, nobody cares. Except me. I am obliged to care, for I understand that this is just another one of His tests. I will submit of course, but I do protest.

So with all due humility, I ask this: Lord, if you wanted to test thy humble servant, don't you think it would have made more sense to design a test I could understand? Who is it exactly who's supposed to be performing the miracle, and what kind of miracle is it? Who do I turn to for guidance? And how do I replace Ivy, my friend, my shining example, and my willing helper? Who will clean and type and organise things now she's gone?

I feel like Moses in front of Pharaoh, urging Aaron to throw down my rod at Pharaoh's feet, where it will turn into a snake so that the Egyptians will witness God's power and, made fearful, they will set us free. But Aaron shakes his head, looks rather embarrassed and shows me his hands, which are empty. 'Damn!' he exclaims. 'I forgot it'. I turn to the crowd, shrug my shoulders and explain: 'Sorry, no snakes today – just can't get the staff.'

The End.